Mary

Labeled In Seattle

Murder by Design: Book 2

Todd Book Publications

LABELED IN SEATTLE

Copyright © 2012 by Mary Jane Forbes
All rights reserved. No part of this book may be used or reproduced by any means, graphic, electronic, or mechanical, including photocopying recording, taping or by any information storage retrieval system without the written permission of the publisher except in the case of brief quotations embodied in critical articles and reviews.

This is a work of fiction. All of the characters, names, locations, incidents, organizations, and dialogue in this novel are either the products of the author's imagination or are used fictitiously. The views expressed in this work are solely those of the author.

ISBN: 978-0-9847948-1-2 (sc)
Printed in the United States of America
Todd Book Publications: 2/1012
Port Orange, Florida

Printer: Lightning Source
Author photo: Ami Ringeisen

ACKNOWLEDGEMENTS

Bouquets of flowers with thanks to the following:

Tasha Hériché. I met Tasha in Newburyport, Massachusetts, and watched her become a beautiful, incredibly computer savvy young woman. She married a handsome Frenchman and they now live with their two adorable children in France where she has embraced her adopted country and its culture. As always, she came to my aid with my story's *French connection*.

Dr. Richard Colton and his wife Connie. Took a reconnaissance trip to Bainbridge, Washington, checking the setting and what had changed since I had been there.

Roger and Pat Grady. Continue to edit, give suggestions, and find inconsistencies, all helping to produce a more polished book.

Lorna Prusak, Molly Tredwell, Vera Kuzmyak. Edited, reviewed, bounced around ideas for the book cover and the escapades of the characters.

*Dear Rick & Connie,
Thank you for your help and support,
Love, Mary Jane*

Books by Mary Jane Forbes

FICTION

Murder by Design, Series:
Murder by Design – Book 1
Murder by Design: Labeled in Seattle – Book 2

The Baby Quilt ... *a mystery!*

Elizabeth Stitchway, Private Investigator, Series:
The Mailbox – Book 1
Black Magic, An Arabian Stallion – Book 2
The Painter – Book 3

House of Beads Mystery Series:
Murder in the House of Beads – Book 1
Intercept – Book 2
Checkmate – Book 3
Identity Theft – Book 4

Short Stories
Once Upon a Christmas Eve, a Romantic Fairy Tale

NONFICTION

Authors, Self Publish With Style

Visit: www.MaryJaneForbes.com for an up-to-date list

Labeled In Seattle

Murder by Design: Book 2

Chapter 1

Paris

The young lady in seat 23A pressed her forehead to the window straining against her seatbelt. A sweeping panorama of Paris lay below as the plane circled Charles de Gaulle Airport. Fourteen hours earlier she was waving goodbye to her parents, grandfather, and best friend Maria Delgado standing behind the Seattle airport window.

Leaning back in her seat she opened her small mirror to check her hair—burnished red, falling around her shoulders. Black lashes fringed green eyes sparkling in anticipation as she wondered about the world she was plunging into, an internship of six months or more arranged by the fashion industry's top employment agency located in Paris.

Gillianne Wilder, now twenty-three, had gone from a barmaid employed at an Indian casino on Bainbridge Island across Puget Sound, to winning a $20,000 fashion design competition, to spending six months in Paris. She gave her family $5,000 of her prize money and banked the remaining $15,000 to fund her trip abroad.

To help bring her dream of being a top fashion designer to a reality, she knew she had to spend time in Paris where the fashion industry began, learning from the best of the best—about fabrics, design techniques, trends, and the business side of setting up her own label back in Seattle. The slight jar of the landing gear locking into place snapped her out of the daydream.

The landing was smooth and upon exiting the plane she was quickly swept along with the other passengers. She ran her hand down her black pant-suit jacket trying to smooth any wrinkles from sitting so long in the cramped plane. Excitement was suddenly tempered with anxiety—French mingled with English, passengers jockeyed for position in the snaking mob heading in the direction of baggage. She hoped.

"Bonjour, Gilly! Here. Here."

Gilly looked around, her eyes scanning the crowd. Where was the voice coming from? She was sure she heard her name.

Strange words bellowed from the ceiling. Saying what?

Oh, God, what have I done?

"Gilly. Gilly."

Her green eyes darted from face to face. Where was the lady?

"Baggage?" Gilly asked a portly woman squeezing around her, sweat discoloring the dress under her armpits.

"Tout droit," the woman replied pointing straight ahead.

The crowd continued moving at a good clip. Gilly clung to her shoulder bag trying not to trip as her heels clicked over the cement. She couldn't veer one way or another if she tried.

"Gilly. Gilly."

The voice was closer. Gilly scanned the people pressing outside the rope calling to friends and family, as well as limo drivers holding signs waiting for their passengers to identify themselves.

There. There was a sign with her name: GILLY. Pushing free of the crush, eyes glued on her name held by a petite, dark-haired French woman waving frantically to get her attention.

"Bonjour, Gilly. Bonjour," the woman called out with a wide smile bobbing up and down as Gilly struggled against the crowd to reach her. The woman thankfully took hold of Gilly's outstretched hand across the rope and pulled her into a warm embrace.

"I'm Gabrielle. You look just like your picture. You have bags?"

"One. I sent two cases of clothes to the apartment address in your email."

"Bon. See that sign? Keep going. I meet you."

"Okay, okay." Gilly's heart was pounding, she struggled to breathe, and her eyes were starting to burn. Take deep breaths, she thought. Straighten up. Focus. Think how you got here—classes at the Seattle Fashion Academy, preparing for the competition, sending your first model down the runway. Think about the moment you were declared the winner. Breathe. You can do this.

Chapter 2

Gabrielle took charge of the situation grasping one of the suitcases, dragging Gilly by the hand, who in turn dragged her rolling suitcase, the tote bag bouncing on her shoulder. Gabrielle flagged down a cab, shouting the address and directing him to put the luggage in the trunk.

"We'll be at the apartment in about twenty-five minutes unless he's really good," Gabrielle nodded in the direction of the cab driver and shooting a reassuring smile at Gilly.

Looking out the window Gilly's first impression was that Paris was a bustling city not unlike Seattle, yet nothing like it at all.

She was greeted with flowering trees, lavender iris, and a profusion of colorful tulips and bushes lining the sidewalks, outdoor cafes and flower stalls. Little cars, which seemed liked toys to Gilly, shot up and down the streets. Buildings were faced with numerous windows most with intricate wrought-iron balconies. The cabbie turned onto a wide boulevard.

"Gabrielle, is that the Arc de Triomphe or are my eyes playing tricks?"

"You are right. You did your homework, Mademoiselle Gillianne. Hang on we are at the traffic circle where a dozen streets converge. It's survival of the fittest, or the bravest," Gabrielle said laughing enjoying the ride with her new client. "We're now on the Champs-Elysées. The side streets can be very narrow. Barely enough for two cars to pass in opposite directions. Such is the case in front of your apartment building. You'll see. A good driver may endure a few scratches, but no dents. If need be, insurance is split fifty-fifty. You've come on a very beautiful day, Gilly. May sometimes is a bit chilly."

"Can we go to a café?"

"Oui. But first you meet your roommates. They're waiting for you. Take a look see at the apartment, which you can do standing in the middle of the living room and turning in a circle. Then, Nicole and Sheridan will join us for an espresso at a nice little café down the street."

Gilly felt herself relax. She was falling in love with Paris and wanted to jump out of the cab to start exploring the shops, buy flowers, and drink the coffee Gabrielle suggested.

Veering to the curb of a white stone building the driver stopped, jumped out and retrieved Gilly's luggage as Gabrielle stepped onto the sidewalk, pulling Gilly by the hand so she wouldn't get out on the street side. Gabrielle asked the fare and counted out the money.

"Merci, monsieur."

"Follow me, Gilly. Your apartment is on the third floor." Gabrielle darted in a big red door, around a corner, and started up the stairs, bumping Gilly's bag on each step. Gilly followed, her bag bumping along in rhythm.

"Is there an elevator?"

"Afraid not, no lift in many apartment buildings. I'm also the agent for your two roommates. There was a third but she left. In tears I might add. Couldn't make it. But that freed up a spot for you. You girls are roughing it with three, but it's cozy and a good deal considering what you said you could afford. And best of all, the metro is at the end of the block and the fashion houses I have you lined up with are all close to a stop—Dior, Chanel, Giorgio, and others."

Stopping on the landing of the third floor, Gabrielle knocked three times flashing a smile at Gilly who was trying to catch her breath.

"A few more times up these stairs and I should be in great shape if I don't have a heart attack first," Gilly said responding to Gabrielle with a smirk.

Gilly heard excited chatter on the other side of the door. "Come on, come on. Pull the blanket over your clothes, hide the mess."

The door flew open and two smiling faces beamed out at Gilly and Gabrielle.

"Come in. Come in." A tall brunette, with a decided New York accent, extended her hand to Gilly. "I'm Sheridan and this is Nicole."

The girls ushered Gilly and Gabrielle into what appeared to Gilly to be a large living room. She would soon see that the couch was really a futon, a small kitchen was behind one side of a partition and three racks on the other side, two full of clothes the third empty. A door led into a small bathroom—salle de'eau they called it with a sink protruding from the wall. All the walls were white, hardwood floor was washed with white paint, four black wrought iron chairs nestled into a table, and all fabric was maroon. Clean and efficient.

Gilly found herself turning in a circle as Gabrielle said but didn't see any beds. "Bedroom?"

"Mezzanine," the three women said together looking up.

Gilly had missed the iron staircase circling up to a loft.

"The landlady was kind enough to store the wall-to-wall king-size bed. Nicole and I found three sturdy cots in a second-hand shop. The foam mattresses are firm. You just have to be careful or you'll trip and the stairs can be tricky before that first cup of coffee in the morning," Sheridan added.

"Welcome to your new home." Nicole, a petite, dark-haired, girl with a French accent, late twenties, stood smiling at Gilly.

"This rack is for your clothes," Sheridan said. "And the dresser behind is yours. Nicole and I found you the mirror over your dresser. As you can see there's no room in the bathroom for our makeup and all the other stuff we girls need. This was a small bedroom but we use it as a large closet."

"The apartment is a pretty good size given your budgets," Gabrielle said. "But it's adequate for sleeping. When you girls make your millions, you'll have fond memories of where you started. Now, is everyone up for a café crème? Our cappuccino with whipped cream, Gilly. My treat."

Gilly was happy to see the girls were wearing jeans with white T-shirts. She hung her jacket on her rack, kicked off her heels and pulled out a pair of red flats.

Trotting down the stairs and out the front door, the three girls chattered filling Gilly in on the neighborhood, pointing to the metro sign, the pharmacie known to Gilly as a drugstore, and a little grocer. They said they'd fill her in on how they work out the food situation and how to get by on as little as possible for meals. They turned the corner and made their way to a small bistro table in front of a café situated in the warm afternoon sun.

An awning with large stripes, blue and red, shielded the café's windows; smaller red umbrellas were anchored through a center hole of the tables not protected by the larger awning. The sidewalk and street were paved with sandstone colored pavers.

"Want me to order my favorite for you?" Nicole asked looking at Gilly.

"Oh, please. My head is whirling. Not sure I could even ask for a glass of water. You do call it water?"

"Close enough, silly," Gabrielle said giving Gilly's arm a squeeze. She then laid open her briefcase and removed a pad of paper and a pen.

A young man approached the table smiling. "Ah, Mademoiselles Nicole and Sheridan, you bring friends."

"Oui, Tony. Meet our new roommate, Gillianne, s'il vous plaît," Nicole said.

"Hi, it's Gilly."

"And I think you've met Gabrielle before."

Gabrielle flashed Tony a quick smile and then looked back at her notepad. Nicole ordered four café crèmes, topped with whipped cream and nutmeg.

Gabrielle handed the top sheet of paper to Gilly. "Here's your schedule for the rest of the week. Do you have the email I sent you? We'll put some names, dates and times on it."

"Yeah, I have it right here," Gilly pulled a folder from her shoulder bag.

"You said you wanted to work from the bottom up so to speak," Gabrielle said. "So the first three weeks will be at the workshops where the clothes are made for one of the fashion houses. You'll start with the group making samples from the designer's sketches, then after the designer okays the construction you'll spend time in patternmaking—how to duplicate a piece for various sizes in the most efficient way, then on to sewing for a few weeks.

"I know you can sew, but that's not the point. You'll learn techniques on how to quickly sew for mass market, refining the methods and techniques for ready-to-wear, and then the finer points of couture. That should round out the first four months."

Tony set four large white cups rimmed in gold containing coffee topped with whipped cream and nutmeg along with two sugars and a chocolate covered almond each, in front of the girls. Gabrielle paid the bill, lifted her cup, and smiled at the three girls. "Here's to a successful internship, Gilly."

Gilly, took a sip. "Wow, that's strong. One of these and I'll be wired all day."

"Believe me," Sheridan said. "You'll need more like three or four a day the way Gabby gets you working."

"Gabby?" Gilly asked. She thought Gabrielle Dupont to be in her early forties.

"Yes, please call me Gabby. I'm not going to tell you anything about your roommates, Gilly, other than to say they are very smart and beautiful, and I'm sure you'll learn a lot from each other. I'd like to be a fly on the wall after I leave you today as they tell you about Paris and the fashion business, and then when you begin to share what happens during the day after you crash for the night in your apartment."

Gabby finished her coffee, made an additional note on Gilly's sheet and handed it back to her. "Sheridan is from the States, New York City, so she knows what it's like to land in a foreign country and not know the language. We have set up a schedule for Wednesday, Thursday, and Friday. One of us will be with you at all times except when you're at work—we'll see you to the door and home again. On Saturday, Sheridan—"

"Gabby, I've switched with Nicole," Sheridan said. "She'll help Gilly on Saturday and I'll take Sunday. A modeling job came up on Saturday."

"Modeling. Gilly, you will be asked from time to time if you'd like to model," Gabby said. "It's always at the last minute when one of the regular models doesn't show. You get paid by the hour—it's a great way to augment your income. Sheridan's lucky. Being five-ten she is frequently asked to fill in. I noted you are five-seven so you'll get a few chances."

"I'm only five-five," Nicole volunteered. "I don't get asked much."

"If it happens, notify your supervisor—they know the routine and will clock you out," Gabby said. "It takes a couple of hours, sometimes three, by the time you report for hair and makeup and a quick fitting."

"Saturday, the sales person for the designer, is expecting a big client so it's a special showing with several models. The fitting generally means a few pins here and there and some double-tape so your boobs don't hang out," Sheridan added with a chuckle.

"Okay, girls, I'm on way back to the office. Gilly, I'll pick you up at seven tomorrow morning. We'll take the metro to your first assignment which is just around the corner from where I work. Here's some money for another round of coffee. And, Gilly … welcome to Paris."

Chapter 3

Two weeks rushed by, each day a blur of new people speaking rapidly in French. Starting in the patternmaking and new design sampling workroom, women took sketches and tried to extrapolate the designer's vision of a piece—cutting a pattern and fitting a sample on a mannequin.

Gilly had already picked up a few new techniques and was quickly adapting to working in a foreign city—if she didn't understand the words she did understand what they were trying to accomplish from the drawings. Nicole and Sheridan tutored her every chance they had when she was with one or the other. Sheridan, having arrived in Paris four months earlier, was particularly helpful with the critical phrases such as understanding directions, ordering coffee, hello—*bonjour*, goodbye—*au revoir*, and the obligatory thank you—*merci*, and please—*s'il vous plaît*.

This morning a fashion house relayed an urgent request for a model for a very special client: five-foot-seven, 127 pounds maximum. She was needed to fill in for a model who called in sick. Gilly was perfect for the assignment and had one hour to whiz through hair and makeup and then twist into the dress. Finished with the beauty end of the preparation, she was rushed into the fitting room and was poured into a long, dark blue velvet gown with a short train.

The woman in charge of three models nipped, tucked, and pushed their bodies into place. "You have five minutes to catch your breath but don't sit down," she told them and dashed to the salon to check when the models should appear. Gilly started down the hallway to the salon passing several rooms occupied by clients standing on platforms being fitted for the garments they were purchasing. Passing one of the doors, a tall blonde, maybe mid-forties stood on the pedestal facing a floor-to-ceiling mirror that wrapped around three walls. The woman's back was to the doorway but Gilly had a clear look at the woman's image in the mirror. Gilly stopped and stared at the woman. Feeling Gilly's eyes the woman looked up catching a glimpse of the girl in the doorway.

Gilly quickly moved on. That was Eleanor Wellington, she thought. I'm sure of it. Skip Hunter, her reporter friend at the Seattle Times had included Mrs. Wellington's picture with her husband in his stories about a gold heist—biggest robbery in Seattle history. Skip said the woman had disappeared with one of Mr. Wellington's employees and it was thought the pair had been in cahoots making off with the gold.

A smile crossed Gilly's face. Just wait until Skip hears I've found his fugitive, she thought. Maybe he'll come to Paris to write more stories on the heist, after all it was a big one, several million dollars if I remember right. I miss Skip. Should've called him. He's probably wondering if I fell off the face of the earth or worse that I love Paris and I'm not coming back. He warned me that might happen before I left. What if he came to Paris to write …

Catching up with the other two models, the first girl was immediately called into the salon. Gilly was the last to enter. The client, a young woman, was putting together a trousseau for her wedding in eight months. She must be from a rich family, Gilly thought. The dress I'm wearing is $3500 and that's without accessories.

Gilly knew that when she was called to model she should listen to the client's comments catching what they liked, didn't like, and why. The modeling assignments provided a wonderful opportunity to hear what the woman buying the clothes thought—insight into the buyer's decision process in picking one dress over another, their comments giving her an advantage in her future designs. After modeling she made it a habit to take a few minutes to write down their impressions. A tingly feeling ran up her spine as she thought again about launching her own label.

The young woman loved the dress Gilly modeled asking her to turn several times, to come closer so she could feel the fabric, and then walk away a few steps to observe how the gown looked from the back.

As Gilly stepped away, following the client's instructions, a tall, dark, and very handsome man passed the open door, walked back into view and smiled at Gilly. Gilly smiled in return, then turned to face the client. The saleswoman thanked her and Gilly exited the room. The other two models had already changed and left the dressing room.

The woman who made adjustments to the gown earlier carefully helped Gilly out of the dress leaving her naked except for her panties. She wondered if she would ever be comfortable with a model's dressing and undressing routine. They were stripped bare naked except for their panties to eliminate any chance of unsightly bumps that would ruin the line of the garments they were modeling.

"Excuse me, mademoiselle."

The male voice came from the open doorway. Gilly grabbed her slacks covering herself as she jumped into the rack of clothes away from the voice. She looked around to see whom he was addressing but the tailor was a madame and didn't pay the slightest attention to the man. Gilly looked straight at the man, brows arched, and was about to tell him to get out when she recognized him as the man who had smiled at her when she was modeling in the salon. The tailor excused herself leaving Gilly alone holding her slacks.

"I'm so sorry," he said. "I didn't mean to barge in but I didn't want to lose you. I'll wait outside." He smiled again and shut the door leaving Gilly peering out from the rack of clothes holding her slacks over her bare chest.

She quickly dressed into her work clothes—black pants, white cotton blouse, and black flats. Her red hair set by the stylist fell in soft waves around her shoulders, and makeup with rosy cheeks and thick black lashes fringing her green eyes remained in place. Slinging her black leather bag over her shoulder she opened the door peering out to see if the man was there.

He was.

"Mademoiselle. I must say your pants were more interesting a minute ago."

"Listen, I don't know what you're doing here, but I have to get back to work. So if you'll excuse me—"

"Let me escort you. Where do you work?"

"No, no, please."

His cologne was light and drifting in her direction as he stepped closer. She was unaware of the animated French chatter from somewhere down the hall.

"I insist."

"Look. I don't know who you are. It's very kind of you to offer to *escort* me to work but I can make it just fine. Now, if you please, mister, let me pass or I shall start screaming for help."

"Ah, mademoiselle, forgive me. I'm too, what you Americans call, pushy. Let's start over. Mademoiselle Wilder, my name is Maxime Beaumont—"

"How do you know my name?"

Monsieur Beaumont smiled down at her. "I should very much like to escort you to work but maybe we can stop for a coffee on the way. If not, then I shall pick you up after you finish work and we shall have a nice quiet dinner at a café around the corner during which we can introduce ourselves properly."

"Hello, Monsieur Beaumont. The package you requested from our legal department is waiting for you at the front desk. I see you found Mademoiselle Wilder." The saleswoman, whose client Gilly had just modeled the gown for, smiled sweetly at the man, and then at Gilly, and then proceeded down the hallway.

"There, you see, I'm not a bad person. Shall we?"

Monsieur Beaumont offered Gilly his arm but she was already heading for the front door.

Chapter 4

Her mind was wandering.

Gilly tried to concentrate on what she was being shown—tricks to patternmaking for various sizes which would then be sent to the cutting workroom. I have to call Skip, she thought. With the time difference it was close to midnight. Iffy that he would still be up. But I spotted Mrs. Wellington, at least it looked like her. I have to tell him right away. I would have called if that *Monsieur* Beaumont hadn't interfered. I shouldn't have let him talk me into a coffee ... but he was so French ... are all Frenchmen so handsome? Dinner tonight? I didn't say yes. He probably won't be waiting for me after I finish...

"What? What was that last step? I'm sorry. Can you show me again, madame, s'il vous plaît? Merci."

Pay attention, Gilly, or your internship will be out the window, she thought chastising herself. The next two hours flew by. Gilly forced herself to concentrate on the patternmaker's every word. "Wonderful. Merci. Merci." Standing back, she smiled at the woman finally grasping the techniques the madame was showing her.

Gilly grabbed her shoulder bag and joined the line to punch out for the day. Waiting her turn, she mulled over the strategy and steps she had learned. Stepping out into the sunshine she headed for the stairs leading down to the metro.

"Hello, Gillianne."

It was Mr. Beaumont, gently grasping her elbow.

"Oh, hi, I didn't think—"

"I know this delightful little café...only a few blocks. All right with you?"

"All right, Mr. Beaumont, but then—"

"Maxime, please," he said with a smile that swept away any notion she may have had about going back to her apartment. As they walked he pointed out places he thought might interest her.

Arriving at the cafe he asked the hostess for a table in the back instead of outside even though the night was mild. More private. Wall sconces with little beaded shades provided a dim light coupled with the soft glow from the table's candles. A pretty, dark-haired French woman stood on the small stage. She was splashed with a beam of light, a love song floating from her bow-shaped red lips. Her lashes fluttered shut as she quietly made love through song to the patrons longing to join her in romance after a day of work.

Gilly looked away from the singer and found Maxime watching her with warmth in his eyes drawing her eyes into his. Seconds passed before she broke the trance. "Tell me, what do you do for work in this beautiful city besides taking an American girl you happened to meet to dinner tonight?" She hoped his work might be a safe subject—cool the warmth in his dark eyes.

Maxime looked away for a moment and then he told her a little about his work as a corporate attorney in a firm his grandfather had founded decades ago. "Very boring, the law. I want to know more about you, Gillianne. Everything about you. Over coffee today you told me you grew up in a little town across the water from Seattle. Puget Sound I believe you said. Now tell me why a beautiful red-haired American girl happens to step into my life in the city of lights." Maxime reached for her hand, lightly kissing her knuckles without taking his magnetic black eyes from her face.

Swallowing, Gilly placed both hands in her lap returning his smile her breathing rapid.

Maxime turned to the waiter as he approached their table. He spoke briefly to the waiter, the order flowing from his lips in French.

"I hope you don't mind my ordering for you. They have a wonderful chicken dish here, very American. We'll explore French cuisine at another time."

Dinner was slow and easy. Gilly began to relax helped along with a lovely white wine. She told him of her ambition to become a famous fashion designer, why she was in Paris, and what she hoped to learn.

Maxime ordered an after-dinner espresso, and then it was time to leave. They walked to his car and he drove her to her apartment. He held her hand as they slowly walked up to the building. The front door was set in an alcove surrounded with roses, their scent filling the mild night air. "You are a very beautiful woman, Gillianne Wilder. Will you have dinner with me again? Next Friday?"

"Yes, I'd like that. It was a lovely night. Thank you."

Maxime gently kissed her cheek. "I'll introduce you to Paris properly with a nice dinner in a beautiful but cozy café and then we'll walk along the Seine. I'll pick you up here, Gillianne. Good night," he said, kissing her other cheek and then left with a slight wave as he got into his car.

Her fingers trembled as she punched in the security code and stepped inside. She heard his car drive away—he had waited until she was safely inside the building. Quietly entering her apartment she took note that Nicole and Sheridan were asleep. Checking her watch, Gilly calculated that with the nine-hour time difference, it was one o'clock in Seattle. Skip should be at work. Gripping her cell phone, her body a little off kilter with Maxime filling her thoughts, she tapped in Skip's code as she stepped into the bathroom closing the door behind her.

"Hey, stranger, how goes it in the city of lights?"

Why did he have to say that? Gilly was suddenly at a loss for words.

"Gilly? You there?"

"Yes, yes I'm here. The city. The city is beautiful. How's Seattle?"

"Rainy afternoon. You caught me with a tuna sandwich at my desk. I hoped you might call sooner. It's been over two weeks since you left. I miss you."

"Miss you, too. I'm learning a lot and … meeting people."

"You sound funny. Are you okay?"

"Yes, of course." Gilly shook her head. Come on girl. Focus. "Saw someone today. A woman. Skip, I'm certain it was your missing Mrs. Wellington. She—"

"Where? Are you sure?"

"I was called to model at this designer's salon for a special customer. Mrs. Wellington was in a fitting room. Her back was to me, but—"

"Then how could you recognize her if you only saw her back?"

"She was facing a mirror, being fitted, as I said. I stared at her for a few seconds but she looked up so I scooted down the hall. But after I modeled I asked the fitter who the woman was."

"And—"

"She said she was a relatively new client. Liked expensive clothes—exquisite taste, her words, exquisite taste."

"Gilly, her name?"

"Elaine Waters."

"EW. That fits. Did you get an address?"

"Heavens no. I wanted to talk to you first. I'll send you an email as soon as we hang up with the name of the salon, street address, and telephone number. Maybe she and her partner in crime fled to Europe. If she's a relatively new client, that tells me she's been to the salon more than once, don't you think?"

"Yes. As soon as I get your email I'm calling Detective DuBois. Gilly, this could be the break we've been hoping for."

Hearing the excitement in Skip's voice, she could visualize him pacing, rubbing his hand over his bald head, blue eyes intense as he processed her words.

Chapter 5

Eleanor Wellington, a.k.a. Elaine Waters, a.k.a. Elizabeth Winters, gazed out of her penthouse window overlooking the carpet of twinkling lights below. In the distance the Eiffel tower glowed piercing the starry black sky. She smiled as her plan to be the soul keeper of her husband's gold bullion crystallized. She had managed to manipulate the fool Gordon Silvers, a.k.a. Glenn Stevens, a.k.a. Gerald Sacco, to flee with her and the crates of gold bullion.

It had been so easy once she realized Sacco and two others—Jack Carlson and Lester Tweed—had pulled off the largest gold robbery in Seattle's history. And there Sacco was, ripe for her picking. She knew with her statuesque body and flowing blond hair that even at the age of forty-five the world was hers. She was sure the fool had killed his two partners in the crime, but she needed proof so that she could never be accused of murder or of having anything to do with the heist. Her part in the whole sordid affair came after the fact, after she found the key to the locker where her ex-lover, Jack Carlson, had stashed the gold the night of the heist double crossing his partners Sacco and Tweed.

Eleanor walked back to the wet bar, poured a quarter flute of champagne and strolled back to the panorama that lay at her feet. She had to be careful not to drink too much, just a little to relax and seduce Sacco, loosen his tongue with liquor—not hard to do. Then she'd get him to tell her the story of how he did away with his partners, all the time being recorded.

Eleanor heard him entering the condo which she had cleverly rented in her new name, Elizabeth Winters. Her slave who followed her every lead, drooling over the fact he had landed the beautiful blonde, set two cases on the floor and quietly walked up behind her, encircled her with his arms and kissed her delicate neck warming the blood in both of their bodies. She leaned back into him accepting his advance and feeling his body harden against her.

"Did you make contact with our buyer?" she asked her words slow and soft.

"Yes, my love. Nineteen of the gold bars are on their way to be melted down and resold—half of the money deposited in our account and the other half here in my two suitcases—one million and eighty-seven thousand dollars. The rest of the gold remains in storage. Want to see the money?"

His hands were now roaming her body as he turned her to look into her eyes, his melting into this goddess like creature.

"Yes. I'd like to see it, touch it. My anticipation for your return was agony but now you're here. I'll come to you in the bedroom. Open the cases while I fix your Manhattan the way you like it—a touch of sweetness with the bitters."

Sacco moaned, his lips grazing her neck down to the wisp of black lace of her peignoir sliding over the black satin gown underneath. Eleanor gently moved from his arms still outstretched to her. She floated to the bar and fixed his drink as he stood transfixed. She looked around at him as she removed a cherry from the silver bowl. Running her tongue over the fruit she then immersed it into the amber liquid.

"Go, Gerald. To the bedroom. Open the cases," she whispered.

Sacco dutifully turned, picked up a case in each hand, and went to the bedroom to wait for her. Eleanor joined him, sitting on the edge of the bed, the cases open on the small bench at the foot revealing stacks of $100 bills. Handing Sacco his drink, a fresh flute of champagne in her other hand, she gazed at the money and smiled. Closing the cases she turned to the besotted man. Yes, this was going to be easy.

Tapping her glass to his, she stood between his legs, leaned in, "Here's to a wonderful life. You are so clever, my dear. Tonight we celebrate the successful culmination of our plan."

Lifting her flute she drained her champagne then nodded to him to do the same. Obliging her suggestion, he plucked the cherry from the glass, laid it on his tongue, swallowed, then drained his glass. Removing her peignoir, she picked up his glass. "Make yourself comfortable, my dear, while I freshen up our drinks."

Leaving the bedroom she heard him turn on the shower. Yes, this was going to be easy.

She quickly mixed a batch of Manhattans in a crystal pitcher, filled her flute with sparkling ginger ale and returned to the bedroom. She turned on the recorder in the bedside table leaving the drawer slightly ajar, checked to be sure the tiny microphone she had stuck to the back of the headboard was still in place, and then lay on the bed smoothing the black satin nightgown flowing around the curves of her body.

Sacco returned to their bed. Eleanor, reclining against the pillows, patted the pillows on his side inviting him to join her. As he glided on the white satin sheets to her side she handed him his drink, again tapped her glass to his, and drank deeply of its contents. Sacco followed her lead.

"I celebrated yesterday, thinking of you once again replenishing our account," she whispered kissing his ear.

"And how did you celebrate?" he asked running his hand down her arm inching closer to the warm black satin.

"I did what all women do. Went to my favorite designer and picked out a few items as well as a fitting for an absolutely exquisite pink silk pant suit. Cost scads of money. It was heaven. Paid in cash so your suitcases full of bills are just in time."

"When will you model it for me?"

Reaching for the crystal pitcher, she refilled his glass. "Oh, in a day or two. But enough of me, my clever man." She tapped her glass to his and took a tiny sip of her drink as he drank two large swallows of his.

"Gerald dear, you must tell me again how you managed the heist. Detective DuBois never suspected you, poor thing, those terrible robbers leaving you bound and gagged in the library."

They both giggled at the scene, Eleanor and her husband coming home from the symphony to find Gerald knocked about by the robbers and leaving him supposedly unconscious on the Persian rug.

"I know DuBois finally came to the realization that Jack Carlson, my husband's former financial consultant, fired financial consultant, was the ring leader. Of course, dearest, I know you must have been the one to so cleverly map out the deed. But they never learned who the third man was. Of course, I immediately, after learning of Jack's death, figured that you had paid the third man to do away with Jack. Really smart."

Sacco leaned back on his pillow, a grin crossing his face. "Yes, it *was* brilliant. Poor Tweed. So stupid. Poor stupid, greedy Tweed. Dumb ass wanted more money to keep quiet. More of *our* money, Eleanor. Of course, I didn't know you were going to find the key to the locker.

Carlson had me scared for awhile. Afraid I wasn't going to find the key. I should have told you about our plans from the beginning, my darling." Sacco leaned over to kiss his love but missed as she turned to fetch the pitcher kissing her shoulder instead. She filled his glass.

So close. So close to his completing the story. Not much longer and she would have her evidence, in his own words.

"Oh, yes, Tweed. I had heard his name. Friend of yours or Jack's?" she asked softly running her fingers along his cheek.

"Jack's. They knew each other in college, but Tweed was always in trouble. He roomed with Jack for awhile. So when we needed another pair of hands to help haul the crates, because we had to hurry you know, Jack suggested Tweed." Sacco drained his drink and held it out to Eleanor for a refill. "Ah, but I used Tweed. He *was* the one who knocked Jack off. Pushed him over a cliff across Puget Sound. Quaint little town. Hansville I believe."

"Oh, you are so smart, Gerald dear, not to get your hands dirty. Is Tweed still around? We wouldn't want him to upset our plans."

"Oh, no. I took care of him. A shot of coke. He had a nasty dog bite on his ankle. He told me an old man's dog bit him. In Hansville. I did him a favor relieving him of his pain. Left him in an ally. No trace. No connection."

Sacco suddenly moved in on Eleanor his glass falling to the floor. He tugged her satin nightgown down from her shoulders pulling her to him, breathing in her perfume, his head slowly slithering to her breast, his eyes fluttering, body relaxed, falling into a drunken sleep.

Chapter 6

Seattle

Skip Hunter, twenty-eight, lead crime reporter for the Seattle Times, sat at his desk staring at Gillianne Wilder's picture tacked to his wall. Another reporter had taken the picture at the Working Girl shop where Gillianne modeled a collection of her designs for the storeowner's show. Gilly was the last model down the red carpet that day. She paused, threw a kiss to the crowd giving her a standing ovation before she darted out of sight behind the blue velvet curtain.

So pretty, he thought. First of her triumphs as a budding designer—her green eyes sparkled at him from the photo, deep red hair circling her face, lips in a bright smile. Those lips. He had tasted those lips. He ached to taste them again, but she had flown off to Paris to learn about the fashion industry where, she said, "fashion was born."

Continuing to tap his pen on his calendar desk pad, his eyes where troubled. Two weeks had lapsed before he had heard from her. Was it his imagination or had Gilly seemed distant when she called to tell him about seeing Eleanor Wellington. It wasn't what she said, more what she didn't say. She was vague. Preoccupied. Maybe she was tired. Maybe he was just tired. Maybe she was lost in thought with all she was learning, or, God forbid, maybe she had met someone. A man.

On the other hand he had heard from DuBois. Once. The detective said he'd get right on Gilly's tip. Contact the Paris police. See if they could turn up Eleanor Wellington. DuBois called back four days later to inform him that a woman by the name of Elaine Waters had visited the salon the day Gilly said. A saleslady picked Eleanor Wellington's photo from five others. However, the trail ended there. They hadn't been able to track her down. Elaine Waters didn't seem to exist. Not in Paris anyway. DuBois said he'd call Skip as soon as he had a lead on the woman.

"Hi, Skipper. Penny for your thoughts."

Caught slouching, Skip snapped up in his chair and looked at the woman who had broken into his thoughts. Dazed for a moment, he looked into the eager brown eyes of Diane Starling, the Times Society Editor.

"Hi, Diane. Sorry, just thinking about one of my stories."

"It's six o'clock. Want to stop for a drink before heading home?" she asked.

Leaning against the frame of his cubicle, he saw a beautiful brunette, her warm eyes and pouty smile inviting him to join her. Why the hell not, he thought. "Sure. Great." He logged off his account, turned off the monitor, and reached for his navy blazer hanging on the hook beside where Diane was standing. His hand swept his buzz cut, a habit from when he shaved his head bald. Since Gilly left Seattle he had let his five o'clock shadow become permanent along with the dark brown fuzz on his head.

"Charlie's okay with you? We can walk. Maybe the night air will sweep away the fog you're in," she said laughing.

Leaving the building, Skip jammed his hands into his chino's pockets. Diane threaded her hand through his arm. They walked in silence. Entering the bar they squeezed around a raucous group and looked for a table. Music flowed from the overhead speakers, glasses clinked, and waitresses in short black skirts and plunging white blouses scurried with trays of drinks to the office workers winding down the day. Spotting two empty stools at the end of the bar, Skip nodded to Diane, took her hand and snaked through the crowd.

Skip ordered a beer. Diane a glass of white wine, "Very cold, please," she said.

Drinks in hand, she touched her glass to his bottle. "Cheers." Her warm eyes beamed over the rim of the glass. "That picture on your wall. You asked me for a copy when we ran it in the paper with the article about that shop's little fashion show. Girl friend?"

"Friend. Only a friend. Her grandfather was a participant in one of my stories."

"I see. And the dog. The picture next to the girl's?"

"Oh, that's my dog all right. Agatha."

"Maybe this wasn't a good idea, Skip. You—"

"No, no. Really. I'm glad you suggested we go out for a drink." He swung around to face her. He saw a woman who wanted to be with him. He touched her fingers holding her glass with the back of his hand. "How's everything going in your society world?" He smiled back at her, letting his body relax. This was exactly what he needed. A drink with a pretty woman. No harm with that.

"Society is heating up with engagement announcements, fall wedding plans, and of course restaurant advertisements—*rent my place for your reception*. Really makes the higher-ups happy with the burgeoning ad revenue."

"How long have you been with the paper? I know you were working here when I started almost three years ago." Skip took a sip of beer suddenly thinking about the day a year ago when he first met Gilly. A bright, fresh, young woman hell bent on being a fashion designer. He didn't realize at the time how captivated he was with her excitement, her excitement for fashion rivaling his own to become a mystery writer, ala Agatha Christie. He had named his Bassett Hound Agatha to keep his dream close.

"Five years. Started as a junior reporter—like you," Diane said. "I remember the day you arrived. My God, you were intense. Still are from what I hear. You wrestled that gold robbery from the lead reporter at that time and now look at you—heading up the crime beat." She bathed him with her smile.

"Yeah. Several lucky pieces of the story came my way. Which reminds me, I have to check in with a detective. Gave him a lead on that gold heist over a week ago."

"I didn't realize the case was still open." Her face fell. Looked as if it was going to be a quick drink. Not drinks and dinner, and…

"Open, but cold." Skip laid a couple of bills on the counter to cover the tab. "Sorry, I have to run."

"Me, too." Diane slid off the stool. "I'll follow you out."

On the sidewalk Skip asked if she parked in the newspaper's garage.

"No. I find it easier to take the bus. Thanks for the drink. Maybe we can do it again sometime?"

"Sure. Stop by," he said with a quick smile.

"I will." To end the awkward silence, Diane planted a very quick peck on his cheek. "Don't work too hard, Mr. Crime Reporter."

Chapter 7

Paris

The workroom was chaotic. Animated chatter flew from sewing station to sewing station. Words spoken so fast Gilly had no chance to translate, catching only a phrase here and there. She forced herself to watch diligently, observing every trick as the hum of the sewing machines going full tilt mingled with the chatter. Fabrics were guided under the foot of the machine, the needles pounding stitches into place. Four weeks had flown by as Gilly observed, discovered, and learned the techniques brought to bear, techniques excellent for one fabric but not another. She was expected to repeat the techniques precisely. No time to make a mistake.

Rumors spread that the fashion house was on the hunt for more elegant fabrics for the holiday season five months away. A buying trip was quickly scheduled to search for new fabrics to produce sample designs for buyers around the world—special orders for discerning buyers demanding something exceptional for their stores, something unique to entice their customers for the holiday parties. They were behind—the unanticipated demand for new elegant fabrics catching the house unprepared. A disaster in the fashion business. Clients were clamoring for sparkle, satins, lace—all form fitting with a hint of a train adding sophistication.

Drama was in.

Gilly was constantly being called to model—her figure, topped with her red hair coiffed into a French twist, or flowing with extensions adding a glamorous element to the glamorous elegant must-have gowns to complete a buyer's stock. Jewels—diamond and ruby earrings, bracelets, necklaces in gold and silver—were worn by the models giving their personal patrons ideas for that special gift from their husbands, or lovers.

Amour filled the air.

More often than not, Maxime caught wind of Gilly's presence in the salon—standing in the doorway with a smile, with a wink of appreciation. Gilly wondered how he knew when she was modeling. Modeling came naturally to her. Showmanship. She slowly turned in front of the client, teasing her with her body language, the gold satin gown's train demurely covering then revealing jewel encrusted strappy silver, gold, or glass-like heels. Catching Maxime in the archway, her heart skipped a beat, heat rising through her body adding a pink glow to her cheeks.

She began checking for possible modeling gigs, and then requesting assignments. The added money was piling up in her bank account, but she really put in the requests hoping to see Maxime and to feel the thrill when he appeared. In the middle of a seam, the needle piercing the fabric, Gilly found herself thinking of him. She waited impatiently for Friday when he would whisk her away for an intimate dinner, waiters hovering around her, topping off her champagne, serving an espresso with a nod from Maxime. Dinner was always followed with a stroll along the Seine sparkling with the reflection of the city lights, moist air caressing her skin, the scent of Maxime's cologne drawing her close.

Last Friday he had turned her into his arms, bringing his lips slowly to hers in a long soft embrace. He had held her close, gazing into her eyes, telling her how beautiful she was in the moonlight.

"Gillianne, Gillianne. My beautiful Gillianne"

Reluctantly leaving the vision of Maxime's embrace, Gilly turned to the saleswoman who was asking her to walk around once more at her client's request.

Friday.

The waiter dressed in black, a white linen towel over his arm, topped her glass with champagne then quietly retreated with Maxime's order for their dinner.

Maxime discreetly took her hand placing it on his knee, covered her hand with his, their table privately tucked behind a bank of large brass pots filled with greenery. A candle flickered on the table playing with the sparkling bubbles of champagne, playing with the soft curves of her little black dress.

Gilly told him of her day and what she was learning in the sewing workroom—how to handle filmy fabrics so they didn't pucker, or the draping of silks and satins to show off the client's form. "I'm scheduled to accompany the lead fabric buyer to Milan next week."

"Must you travel with her or can you meet her there?" Maxime lifted her hand to his lips.

"Well, I presume I'll travel with her—I don't know where we're going, and then the language, and—"

"Gillianne, I want to steal you away, to be with you, just us. May I suggest you accompany your teacher to Milan, visit the fabric mills, then beg off for a weekend to play tourist. I will be your guide and fly you back to Paris Sunday evening. Please, say you will allow me to show you the sights of Milan, and especially the pleasures of the Italian cuisine."

"Umm, sounds wonderful. And, I won't 'beg off.' I'll just tell her I'm staying with a friend."

"What day next week is this scheduled trip?" Maxime looked at her with such warmth, Gilly wished they were in Milan this minute.

"Tuesday. Tuesday morning were flying out. I guess it's a little over an hour nonstop?"

"Yes, and when can I have you?"

"She said we'd fly back Thursday afternoon. Maxime, can you really get away?"

"My darling, I won't allow anything to interfere."

Chapter 8

Early morning sunshine warmed the Paris air as the three roommates settled at their favorite outdoor bistro table for a quick café crème before heading to work.

"You're taking a dream trip to Milan," Sheridan said accepting her coffee from the waiter. "How ever did you land it?"

"I kept badgering Gabby that I wanted to accompany a buyer looking for fabric—what textile factories she visited, names of the best contacts, and how she went about making her choices. Somehow she got wind of the fashion house, where I'm interning, preparing to make a quick reconnaissance for holiday fabrics. They had a rash of inquiries about their holiday line and wanted to offer more of a selection to their clients. I was in the right place at the right time with the right badgering," Gilly replied with a quick laugh, eyes wide.

"What time does your flight leave tomorrow, and when do you expect to be back? Dinner Thursday so you can tell us all about what you saw? Make us jealous?" Nicole asked sipping her coffee.

"I'm meeting the buyer at the airport. Flight leaves at 12:20. Our last appointment is Thursday at 1:00, and she is returning soon after."

"She's leaving? What does that mean? You're not flying back with her?" Sheridan asked.

Gilly clutched her small cup then looked up at her friends with a bright smile, her eyes crinkling at the corners with excitement. She was ready to divulge that Maxime was going to meet her, show her Milan, and that they were flying back together on Sunday afternoon.

"You know I've been seeing a man. A Frenchman."

"Yes. Nicole and I didn't want to pry. Are you finally going to tell us who this mystery man is and how you met him and—"

"His name is Maxime. He spotted me at my first modeling assignment and immediately took over tourist duties showing me Paris, wining and dining, literally. Sometimes he picks me up for lunch if I can get away, but we meet every Friday night—winding down the work week on a high note as he would say."

"Wow. What's his last name? What does he do?" Nicole leaned forward, anxious to hear about the man, her eyes showing concern.

"Beaumont, Maxime Beaumont. He's a corporate attorney in a firm his grandfather founded."

"Have you checked him out?" Nicole asked not responding to her friend's excitement over this Monsieur Beaumont.

"Check him out? What do you mean? He's definitely an established lawyer, a well-to-do lawyer. You should see how the waiters fawn over him. The staff at the salon defers to him, making sure whatever he asks for he gets."

"I'm just worried about you, honey," Nicole said reaching out to squeeze Gilly's hand. "A Frenchman, handsome, attentive, and wealthy can turn a girl's head. Frenchmen fall in and out of love every hour, I swear. And here you are, a beautiful young woman, in the city of love, in the springtime where amour springs from every fresh new flower."

"I appreciate your concern." Gilly reached out to grasp her friend's hands. "Honestly, I do. I want you to be happy for me. I don't know what this means for me. Who knows, Nicole, maybe I'll end up staying in Paris."

"Back to my question," Sheridan said smiling. She didn't share Nicole's skepticism only wishing she had met the Beaumont guy first.

"Maxime wants to introduce me to Milan, show me the sights, and experience the food. He's taking me to see da Vinci's painting of the Last Supper. Attend a wine tasting to learn about Italian wines. See the churches, museums, and maybe take a day trip to Monaco."

"Gilly, are you aware he may have more than food and wine on his mind?" Nicole said in a low voice.

Hesitating, Gilly looked from Nicole to Sheridan. "I know it's sudden. I keep asking myself if he's real ... if my feelings for him are real."

"So?" Sheridan asked.

"I ... if ... he's all I can think about. If he says he loves me ... do you think I'm wrong?" Gilly whispered. She looked at her friends, questioning, seeking their advice but knowing deep down it didn't matter what they thought.

Chapter 9

Monaco

The yacht's captain gave the command to the crew to pull up anchor. The sleek vessel slowly pulled out of the bay leaving Monaco's bikini-clad sunbathers and pristine beach glistening in the afternoon sun. The woman, who had chartered the captain and his ship the Lady Margaret for a week's vacation out at sea, and her companion were lounging on the afterdeck.

Elizabeth Winter's, formerly Elaine Waters, formerly Eleanor Wellington felt the lecherous eyes of Gordon Silvers, formerly Glenn Stevens, formerly Gerald Sacco. The pair was of an age. The difference being she felt she was royalty and deserved the attention she received and if truth be told enjoyed the lascivious glances of the opposite sex. Indeed, she did everything to attract the glances—kept her body firm and oiled and her clothes revealing. So it was at this moment—Eleanor lying on the chaise lounge, her bikini a mere string across her breasts and another around her loin. Her filmy caftan open, draped to the side.

She enjoyed Sacco's attention this late afternoon as the ship gathered speed heading out to sea, the wake churning behind.

Watching the water convulse to each side as the ship cut through the water, Sacco's blood began churning as well. The sun soon dipped below the horizon and a full moon rose from the east as dusk merged into night.

"Madame, cocktails are ready in your stateroom as you instructed," the ship's steward announced. "What time and where do you wish dinner to be served?"

"Late, maybe ten o'clock, out here on the deck. And, please inform the captain that I don't wish him to drop anchor for the night until after midnight."

"Very good, madame."

"Well, Gerald, would you like to join me for cocktails?" Eleanor, plucked a slice of orange from the fruit tray, slowly lowered it to her mouth, her lips licking the sweet nectar.

Sacco popped up from his chair. Yes, he wanted to join her for cocktails and for other activities between cocktails and dinner. He envisioned a truly glorious happy hour.

Rising from the chaise Eleanor stretched her arms over her head and then slowly ambled inside. She wanted to verify some information Sacco had given her about the gold bullion by slowly acquiescing to his advances in the ship's elegant bedroom. The steward had just confirmed the happy-hour delicacies she had ordered to be brought to the cabin at eight o'clock were in place. Her evening plans were now set in motion.

"Gerald dear, did you inform our gold seller that we'd be contacting him to liquidate all the gold bullion after our vacation? We can't trust the spot price for gold will continue to increase."

"Yes, my love. He is expecting us. I like your plan to be rid of the bars. He will deposit the money equally in the ten accounts we set up."

"Good. Once we leave the bullion behind there will be no way of tracing it back to us. It will simply vanish, melted down, recast into other bars for sale to unsuspecting buyers and jewelers around the world."

Twice Eleanor rang for additional liquor, and wine. At ten o'clock she strolled to the deck followed by Sacco stumbling after her. It had been a wonderful evening and he looked forward to more of the same after dinner. Actually he was a little irritated that dinner interrupted their activities. But whatever the woman wanted was okay because she certainly was accepting of his amorous advances.

The night was balmy, the stars bright, the deck cozy with tapered white candles glowing in glass hurricane covers. Tiny votives flickered on a table between the two chaise loungers. The steward poured red wine from a large carafe and set an antipasto platter between the pair, and later served the main course of veal medallions and cubes of red potatoes sautéed in butter and chives.

"Cheers, my dear," Eleanor said. "Here's to a safe journey."

Gerald gulped his wine. "You know, at first when you suggested a little getaway on this boat, I wasn't sure it was such a good idea. I can't swim, as I told you. Actually, water scares me. But, today you put those fears behind me." Sacco finished his wine, and refilled the glass. He nodded to Eleanor. "Can I top off your glass, my love?"

"I'm fine, thank you. You go ahead. Finish it if you like."

Tapping her glass, he delivered his toast. "Here's to tomorrow. May it be exactly as today."

The steward silently appeared, removed the main course plates and set a small plate of pastries on the table along with two tulip-shaped brandy glasses and a bottle of cognac.

"Thank you. That will be all for tonight," Eleanor said softly, smiling at the steward.

"Very good, madame. Enjoy your evening," he said disappearing into the ship.

Sacco hadn't noticed that she only sipped her drink—her wine, the cocktails before, the afternoon's wine with lunch.

Eleanor watched him closely.

It was almost time.

During the afternoon, behind sunglasses, her eyes sought the lowest railing, the best concealed spot where one might accidentally fall overboard. Especially someone who had enough alcohol in his body to render him unconscious. She had strolled the afterdeck checking windows where one might have a vantage point of the low bars if passing by inside.

She had found the perfect spot.

It was time.

"Gerald, you look a little peaked. Let's stand by the rail so you can get some breeze, cool you off. You'll feel better. Perk you up. The night is young."

"Yes ... I don't feel too good."

"Here, lean on me, dear."

"You're so strong, Eleanor."

Sacco wrapped his arm over her shoulders for support. She laid her head against him, her arm tight around his waist, holding him up, preventing him from keeling over, guiding him to the rail, the rail she had spotted earlier.

He leaned into the rail.

"Here, lean out so you feel the breeze," she whispered.

The air was soothing to his skin.

He leaned further.

"Ah, yes." Sacco let her put his foot on the first rung of the railing.

He leaned out.

His hand slipped.

He reached for her clutching nothing but air as his body slid over the rail into the sea.

Thirty minutes passed as the Lady Margaret continued on her course away from land.

Eleanor rang for the steward from the stateroom.

"Gerald hasn't come in and I'm dreadfully tired. Will you round him up and bring him to our stateroom. I'm afraid he's had too much to drink."

Chapter 10

Monaco

Skip Hunter had just spent eighteen grueling hours flying from Seattle to Paris after receiving the call from Seattle Detective Mirage Dubois. Thanks to Gilly's tip, Paris Police Detective André Boisot had located Eleanor Wellington following her winding trail through two aliases. Each bend in the trail had led to her companion Gerald Sacco.

The search for Wellington and Sacco had taken five weeks but Boisot's diligence finally paid off. Eleanor had rented a Paris condo under the name of Elizabeth Winters. The condo manager had positively identified Winters as Eleanor Wellington and her companion, Gordon Silvers as Gerald Sacco. They had always maintained the initials EW and GS.

Boisot then scheduled officers to stakeout the condo, trailing the pair's every move as they individually went about their daily business, holding off an arrest until one or the other led them to the stash of forty-five million dollars worth of gold bullion.

Dubois had informed Skip that the pair was finally under surveillance and had invited Skip to tag along with him to Paris to witness the arrest. DuBois knew Hunter was chronicling the heist hoping to write an expose, a novel to start a new career as a mystery writer. If he could arrange it, Skip would witness the pinch. DuBois and Hunter had boarded a plane at Seattle's SeaTac Airport within two hours of receiving the information from Detective Boisot that Wellington and Sacco were to be arrested.

Skip had another reason to travel with DuBois to Paris, one he did not share with the detective. Gilly. His unease had grown over the weeks since Gilly called with the Wellington tip. Maybe if he saw her, held her hand … hell, he had to hold her in his arms. Then and only then would he be able to ease the knot in his stomach. The knot forming from the fear she had moved on, away from him … or had met someone else.

Skip tried to sleep on the second leg of the journey, nighttime over the Atlantic Ocean, but he couldn't quiet his mind. He kept going over the events that had put him in the middle of the gold robbery investigation, had brought him onto this airplane, this night. From the beginning he felt the man's body found on the shores of Puget Sound in the little town of Hansville was a victim of murder. No one agreed with him at the time. They all said it was an accident. Everyone that is except Gilly and her grandfather, Clay Wilder. Gramps. That was how he met the redhead, a woman who wanted to be a fashion designer, and not any fashion designer, but one with her own label and someday head of her company, House of Gillianne—fashions for the career woman.

Skip closed his eyes and smiled at the vision of the eager, driven girl he met that day. Of course, he was just as driven to become a writer. Even named his dog Agatha Christie, but he soon learned that that wasn't so strange as she had named her tabby cat Coco. Coco Chanel.

DuBois' head slid down onto Skip's shoulder. Skip let him sleep.

Closing his eyes again, he smiled at the picture of his editor breaking and running the story under Skip's byline after Skip had a received a tip that the man on the beach was a former financial consultant to Wellington. It turned out that the dead man on the beach was probably the ringleader of the heist. But through a strange turn of events, which Skip wasn't quite sure of, Wellington's wife Eleanor had disappeared at the same time Gerald Sacco disappeared, Wellington's property manager. The authorities were certain the pair had made off with the gold and now Wellington was chomping at the bit for its return. And, he didn't care if his wife went to jail, in fact, at this moment he relished the thought of her spending years behind bars for betraying his love.

Skip hoped he could catch up with Gilly, but when they landed the next morning at Charles de Gaulle Airport they were met by the Paris police and were whisked away on a police jet for the hour-and-half trip to Monaco. Boisot's men had lost Wellington and Sacco but scrambled and had picked up their trail again in Monaco. Gilly would have to wait.

They were told the plane would be met by the Monaco authorities. The pair in question had contracted for the captain and his yacht, the

Lady Margaret, for a week's getaway, but a little after midnight the captain had radioed the shore that a man was overboard, lost at sea. The man's companion, a woman, was distraught and the captain had turned the yacht around and was heading back to Monaco.

Boisot bumped down the jet's aisle and sat across from DuBois and Skip. They discussed the use of the various aliases of the wanted pair and decided to use, initially, the names they had used when boarding the yacht. DuBois and Hunter would stay out of sight until they were ready to accuse Eleanor of making off with the stolen gold bullion. Boisot handed them hooded rain slickers in the event Eleanor was on deck.

The plane landed in Monaco and Boisot and DuBois, followed by Skip, hustled down the stairs to the group of officers standing on the tarmac. They were escorted to a police vessel moored at the dock waiting for the men's arrival. Within thirty minutes they pulled alongside the Lady Margaret.

The captain met the officers as they boarded.

"I informed Mrs. Winters that the Monaco police wanted to question her about the disappearance of her companion."

"That's all you told her, right?" DuBois asked.

"Yes. She's in her stateroom. Do you want the steward to inform her that she's wanted in the main cabin?"

"Yes," Boisot said. "This is how I want to handle the situation. I and the Monaco police officers will question her first about the missing Mr. Gordon Silvers. During this session, one of your crewmen will take Detective DuBois and a Monaco officer to search her room. We do not want Elizabeth Winters to see DuBois so make sure your crew member understands that. It is very important."

"What about this man. Your name?" the Monaco detective asked.

"Skip Hunter. I'm here on background—"

"He's with me," DuBois said. He and Skip had already decided not to talk about his being a reporter unless asked. Skip didn't want any of the officers to hold back fearing their names would appear in print. "I'd like Mr. Hunter to be present during the questioning of Mrs. Winters. Not in the room mind you, as she may recognize him from working on our case prior to her disappearance. I'm sure you're going to record her statements, but Mr. Hunter wants to hear her voice, how she handles herself." DuBois already equipped Skip with a high-powered receiver to put in his ear.

The officers took up their positions so all Eleanor saw as she was escorted into the main cabin was the Monaco detective and one of his men. Wringing a damp handkerchief in her clenched fist, Eleanor occasionally dabbed a tear from her eye as she related the prior day's events: her companion's heavy drinking, her going to bed, her concern over his not joining her, and then her call to the steward to find her companion. When he was not to be found she surmised he must have fallen overboard. She said the Lady Margaret's captain told her he had notified the Monaco authorities that a man was apparently lost at sea and that they would circle with flood lights to try to find the man.

DuBois joined Skip in the hall outside the cabin, tapped him on the shoulder indicating he wanted to talk to him. Skip followed DuBois back to Eleanor's stateroom where a recorder laid on one end of a dresser under a large mirror. A bouquet of lilies in a crystal vase sat on the other end.

"Skip, we found this cassette in Mrs. Wellington's purse, on the floor tucked under the bed. She probably didn't want to take any chances on losing it. Take a listen."

Dubois pushed the button and a very drunk Sacco slurred out the participants in the gold heist and a detailed description of how they pulled it off. He talked about a man named Lester Tweed, a man Skip had learned was connected to the dead man on the beach. Later Tweed had turned up dead in an ally. Sacco confessed to the part he played in the heist, and that he had killed Tweed.

At the end of the recording, DuBois turned off the machine. DuBois and Skip looked at each other—so it appeared Eleanor had done away with Sacco and believed the forty-five million was now hers and hers alone.

Not satisfied with his initial search, Boisot grunted as he tore Eleanor's purse apart. A smile spread across his face as he recognized a name written on a piece of paper in a small compartment of Eleanor's bag. It was the name of a money launderer, and a fence for stolen jewels and gold. A man he had been trying to nail for years.

Boisot led the way back to the main cabin where the Monaco detective was questioning Mrs. Winters. When they entered the cabin, Eleanor was in the middle of a crying spell. Her eyes immediately riveted on DuBois and Skip, bouncing from one to the other.

DuBois laid the recorder on the coffee table and pushed the play button. Eleanor stared at the small machine. DuBois and Skip stared at her while the other lawmen switched back and forth—recorder to the pale woman and back to the recorder.

Eleanor did not go quietly. At first denying everything but when DuBois played the cassette again asking her to confirm the woman's voice on the tape was hers, she turned violent. Cursed at the officers, tried to run out of the room but was stopped. Picking up a crystal vase she threw it at DuBois. The vase bounced off of him, smashed against a brass rail spewing shards of glass. DuBois received a scratch on his arm but Skip, standing next to the rail suffered a deep gash on his cheek.

Eleanor suddenly froze in place. She pulled herself tall, nose in the air, and allowed the officers to cuff her. They hauled their prisoner to shore where Boisot made arrangements for her transportation to a Paris jail awaiting the proper documents to remand her to Seattle under the care of Detective DuBois. The Monaco police suspected her of killing her companion but withheld charging her until forensics dusted the yacht and the Coast Guard searched for the body. Boisot immediately contacted his officers in Paris to bring in the man named on the paper in Eleanor's purse. The gold was still missing.

Detective DuBois charged Eleanor as an accomplice in the theft of the gold bullion. "A stiff prison sentence awaits you, Mrs. Eleanor Wellington, if not the death penalty for the murder of one Gerald Sacco."

Chapter 11

Milan

"Hotel Principe di Savoia, per favore." Gilly slid into the backseat of the cab as the driver deposited her suitcase in the trunk, drove away from the curb and began weaving through the afternoon traffic. Pulling to a stop in front of a creamy five-story building, the Savoia hotel rose in front of her. The driver jumped out, retrieved her bag and handed it to a bellman. Gilly paid the driver and followed the bellman into the spacious, opulent lobby filled with greenery, and marble tile.

The man across the counter took her name, scanned the registration list, and gave the room number and card key to the bellman. Smiling at Gilly, the attendant wished her an enjoyable visit at the Savoia.

A ride on the elevator, and a short walk down a hallway, the bellman opened the door to her suite.

Stepping into a room of red and gold, with gleaming walnut furniture Gilly thought the room must be meant for royalty. At the very least the rich and famous.

The bellman put her suitcase in a room off to her right and left the suite closing the door behind him.

She stood in the center of the room with warm red walls and red drapes trimmed with lush gold fringe. A couch and two facing chairs upholstered in red and gold stripe damask were separated by a coffee table inlaid with ivory. Turning slowly she saw paintings in gilded frames, bronze wall sconces, and red roses in a crystal vase on an inlaid antique sideboard.

Walking to the room where the bellman had taken her suitcase, she gasped at the beauty of a luxurious bedroom with creamy wainscoting topped with delicate peach walls. Drapes in peach and gold silk framed the windows. Two delicate walnut chairs were padded with peach and gold tapestry. Matching throw pillows lined the top of the large king-size bed the bedspread matching the drapes. A small bouquet of white roses sat on a small round table between the two antique chairs. Across the room was a large walnut armoire.

Gilly laid her purse on the bed and slowly wandered back to the sitting room taking in the elegance of the suite. There was a light tap on the door from the adjoining room. Maxime opened the door and entered her suite.

"Gillianne, finally, you arrive."

He placed a quick peck on her cheek, picked up the phone and gave instructions to the person on the other end of the line. She recognized the word champagne and presumed they were going to enjoy a glass before going out for dinner.

Hanging up the phone, Maxime turned to her, briefly closing his eyes. "Beautiful, beautiful, my little bird."

He gently lifted her chin, gazed into her eyes, his dark orbs penetrating her green, and slowly kissed her lips.

"You must be tired after all that traipsing around in warehouses. Why don't you freshen up? My room is part of the suite so I'll do the same. Our tray of goodies will be here soon." Releasing her he returned to his room leaving the connecting door open.

Gilly's eyes followed him as he left, her body weak from his embrace. Returning to her bedroom the shafts of afternoon sun seemed to float through the filmy curtains turning the walls and satin spread into warm golden hues. Gilly felt like a fairy princess in the elegant surroundings. Not knowing where Maxime had in mind for dinner she took a quick shower and then slipped into a short white silk organdy dress with tiny straps made of sparkling diamond-like stones. A pair of silver strappy heels completed the outfit. Taking a look in the mirror, she hardly recognized herself—her cheeks were flushed, her eyes sparkled, her red hair seemed to be on fire—she felt wonderful.

Stepping from the dressing into the sitting area of the magnificently appointed suite, Maxime was just popping the cork of the champagne bottle as the door closed behind the waiter. She approached him with a tentative smile.

"I wasn't sure where you were taking me for dinner … am I dressed appropriately?"

"My darling, you are perfect. How beautiful you are." Turning back to the champagne he poured the sparkling liquid into the crystal flutes.

Handing her one, he tapped his to hers. "Here's to our time together. I shall introduce you to Milan like no woman has seen it before."

With the setting sun shadows crept into the room and Maxime lit the candles on the table between them. She sat in one of the gilded chairs sipping her champagne and told him of her adventures at the textile mills and how the buyer she was with explained the different fabrics and how to discern the quality weaves, textures, and threads from the poor. He sat opposite her, enchanted, sipping his champagne as he listened to her excitedly describe the elegant fabrics she had seen, nothing like she had ever seen before. Finishing their champagne he told her of the tour he had planned for the next two days. Setting his glass on the table, he pulled her gently to her feet and into his arms. His lips touched her cheek with a tender kiss.

"Are you ready for dinner?" he asked smiling.

"Yes, and I warn you I'm starving," she replied kissing his cheek in return.

Strolling into the hotel's elegant dining room filled with candles and soft music, the waiter led them to a private table in the garden. Over dinner, he more than once raised her hand to his lips, answered her questions about the Italian people and their customs.

He told her he had summered with his mother on a stretch of the coast where it curves between the villages of Amalfi and Positano."Maybe we can have a holiday in Positano sometime?" he said, again raising her hand to his lips.

After dinner they returned to the suite. A carafe of coffee and a bottle of brandy had been placed in the sitting area and the staff had lit several candles throughout the room.

Entering the warm glow Gilly turned into Maxime's arms wanting to feel his lips on hers.

Responding to her, he enfolded her into a warm embrace.

"My darling, you are so beautiful."

Picking her up, he carried her to the bedroom and laid her on the bed. The covers had been turned down, the bed welcoming them. He doffed his jacket, loosened his tie. He removed her shoes and laid next to her pulling her to him. Her arms encircled his neck, he slowly lowered his lips to hers. The kiss was warm, then hot, then urgent.

"Gillianne, my beautiful songbird." He carefully slid the glittery crystal straps off her shoulders, reaching around he pulled down the zipper letting the dress fall below her bare breasts.

"Maxime, I—"

"Shhh, don't talk. I want to look at you, to touch you, to have you look into my eyes and say you want me, too. Please, my little bird."

Quickly removing his clothes, he knelt beside her. Slowly her clothes fell to the floor and slower still he caressed her body, felt it quiver under his touch, convulse and arch to his kisses. He felt her wince as he took her. "My little bird, I love you."

"Maxime."

"Yes, it's your Maxime. Cry out my name, now, now my beauty."

"Maxime, Maxime, Maxime!"

~ ~ ~

The following days swept by—they talked, they laughed, the wind blew in her hair as he drove through the city showing her the sights, and they made love.

In a rented Porsche he drove the curves of the hills that sprang from the water lining the coast. They spent three hours in Monaco then began the drive back. The car climbing, climbing, climbing to a perch with grass and shade trees. He laid out a blanket and produced a picnic lunch—wine and cheese and baguettes of thick, chewy, golden Italian bread—on the crest of the hills looking over the sparkling blue Mediterranean Sea.

Then it was time to return to Milan.

Their last night.

Saturday night.

Maxime ordered champagne and dinner to be served in their suite followed with coffee laced again with fine brandy, and then he made love to her.

Gilly was in a dream and never wanted to wake up. Maxime had anticipated and attended to her every desire.

The world outside had ceased to exist.

Chapter 12

Paris

Maybe she isn't home.

Standing on the sidewalk in front of Gilly's apartment building, Skip shifted from one foot to the other. He looked up at the windows. He locked his fingers on top of his head then let them fall to his side expelling a breath. She'd said the apartment was on the third floor. What did he expect? A sign in the window, *Gilly's up here.*

He'd tried a few times from Monaco to reach her on her cell phone but she didn't pick up. He'd only left one message telling her he was in Monaco and hoped he would be able to see her in Paris before he changed planes for his return flight to Seattle.

She hadn't called him back.

On the other hand, maybe she was home. In which case he would wrap her in his arms, then throw her over his shoulder and cart her back to Seattle. Yeah, like that would happen ... not. What's the matter with you, Hunter? I'll tell you what's the matter. She's infused herself into all your thoughts, hell, into your heart. Stop it. Don't just stand here. Ring the bell for God's sake. Find out if the woman's there.

Skip marched up to the door and pressed the button for her apartment.

"Âllo, oui? C'est qui?

"English, please?"

"Hello, yes? Who is it?"

"Skip Hunter. Is Gillianne Wilder there?"

"One moment."

Skip waited, rocking back and forth—toes to heels to toes.

The door opened and a young woman about Gilly's age, long wavy black hair, dark eyes, peered out at him. "Hello, monsieur. I'm sorry but Gillianne isn't here."

Skip let out a deep sigh. His head dropped. He looked back at the woman. "Is she coming back soon? I left her a message a couple of days ago. I told her I was wrapping up a story in Monaco and hoped to stop by on my return to Seattle. But—"

"Oui, Seattle. Come in. Come in. She has mentioned her friend Skip. Please forgive me. I'm Nicole, Gilly's roommate." Nicole stuck out her hand and grasped his. "Come, meet Sheridan. Time for coffee at the café?" she asked.

"Sure. Sure." Skip followed Nicole up the stairs taking two steps for every one of hers.

"Sheridan, look who's here … for Gilly?" Sheridan dropped a magazine to the floor catching Nicole's wide-eyed look of panic. "This is Skip Hunter. Gilly's friend … from Seattle."

"Oh. Oh. Gilly's not here."

"So I've been told." Skip's eyes narrowed.

"I'm Sheridan Cunningham, New York City."

She too offered to shake his hand.

"Nice to meet you … both of you, but—"

"Would you care for a café crème, a cappuccino, at our café around the corner? It's the least we can do after you've come all this way." Sheridan said.

"He said he would … I already invited him," Nicole said panic showing in her eyes under her raised brows.

"Great, great," Sheridan sputtered. "Well, you can see our apartment—just turn your head left, right and up at the loft. It's not very big but none of us are home that much. There are three cots … with mattresses as you can see up there."

"You're right … it is compact," Skip said with an easy smile. "I know Gilly is banking all she can, at least that's what she said before she left. She wants to go into business when she comes back to Seattle in a few months. Start her own clothing line. Are you two designers?"

"Wannabes." Nicole grabbed her shoulder bag. "Come on, Skip, we'll chat at the café. It's a beautiful day for a coffee with a friend of Gilly's … from Seattle."

He certainly caught the two off guard—both lounging in shorts, T-shirts, and flip-flops, jeweled flip-flops. Skip felt some tension when Nicole had introduced him to Sheridan and both girls seemed flustered.

They were very pretty. Sheridan was almost his height. Still, they didn't seem to know what to do with him.

Skip got a kick out of Nicole when they sat down at the little table outside the café, especially her rapid-fire French ordering the coffee. He took a sip of the café crème placed in front of him. "Very nice and very strong," he said smiling at the roommates, his shoulders easing a bit.

"Did Gilly know you were going to be in Paris?" Sheridan asked.

Nicole turned her head quickly to Sheridan jerking back to Skip waiting for his reply.

"Not really. As I told Nicole, I'd left her a message but she hasn't called back. That was two days ago."

"Gilly is in Milan," Nicole said. She looked at Sheridan, back to Skip and continued. "She had a terrific opportunity. One of the fabric buyers was going to Milan and invited Gilly to accompany her. Gilly said the designer wanted the buyer to find more samples for her holiday line. Gilly was very lucky because we don't often get that kind of opportunity."

"Of course, she had hounded our agent to find her such an opportunity," Sheridan added.

"Sounds like my Gilly. That probably explains why she didn't return my call. When do you expect her back? This afternoon? I can—"

"Oh, oh, no ... not until late, very late today," Nicole said almost in a whisper.

Sheridan closed her eyes. What were they going to say? Certainly not the whole story. Skip saw Sheridan close her eyes, holding her breath, then she opened her eyes piercing his.

"Well, I'm sorry I missed her. I'm traveling with a detective from Seattle. Our flight leaves in a couple of hours so I have to get to the airport." The girls were hiding something. He wasn't sure what but he thought he detected the two sighing in relief, even smiling at him ... not a pinched smile like in the apartment. It was part of his job as a reporter to be aware of body language, the vibes a person gives off when he's interviewing them.

Gilly in Milan on business but not returning until today ... late. She's with a man, he thought. I can feel it. My God, am I losing her ... so soon ... so quickly? Well, nothing I can do here, but when she returns to Seattle that will be a different story. I never told her how much I care about her. Care? Hell, I'm in love with her. There it is. Right there out in front of me. I don't know who this guy is, but I'll win her back. At least I'll try to.

Skip threw some bills on the table to pay for the coffee. The roommates protested, but Skip told them it was his treat and thanked them for taking the time to meet with him.

"Maybe Gilly will give me a call when she gets back to Paris. Please tell her that because of her tip the police arrested the bad guys or, in this case, the bad woman."

Chapter 13

Less than two hours ago Gilly was in Milan, in Maxime's arms, and now she was back in Paris. Maxime helped her into a cab in front of the airport, gave her apartment address to the driver, and paid the fare with a generous tip.

"I'll see you Friday, darling?" he asked tossing her green silk jacket onto the seat next to her and folding the filmy silk of her strapless sundress inside the cab door.

Gilly nodded, yes, looking up at him from the backseat, running her fingers over his hand gripping the car door. So handsome—sunglasses, black hair, black turtleneck, black pants, black shoes.

"I love you" he whispered kissing her palm before shutting the door. She waved goodbye as the cab merged with a line of cars leaving the airport.

Paris was beautiful, more brilliant than when she had left for Milan only a few days ago. She laid her head back against the seat, raised her hand to her cheek, closed her eyes and for a moment she was in Maxime's arms.

"Mademoiselle. Mademoiselle, we're here."

"Merci." She grasped the handle of her suitcase the driver had placed on the sidewalk and slowly strolled to the door of her building. The night was serene in the glow of the street lamp—traffic was light even for a Sunday evening. The air was cool in the hallway sheltered from the day's heat.

Gilly inserted her key in the apartment's door, hesitated a moment before stepping back into the real world, her real world, then she pushed the door open.

"Gilly, we missed you." Nicole jumped up and hugged her roommate. Sheridan grasped the suitcase from Gilly's hand and led her friend inside closing the door.

Gilly blinked in the brightly lit room. Shutting her eyes, she inhaled the apartment's familiar scent. Snapping her eyes open, she smiled at her friends. "What a nice homecoming."

"We want to hear everything about Milan. Come, we don't care if you're tired, let's go to the café for a coffee," Nicole said. Snatching her purse, she turned Gilly around and back out the door, jerking her head at Sheridan to hurry along.

Stepping quickly down the stairs, Nicole stole a furtive glance at Sheridan. Both girls shared a wide-eyed glance. They feared the worst had happened. Love and surrender were written all over Gilly's face, and her body language screamed seduction.

The girl's chattered about the lovely Sunday evening, that is Nicole and Sheridan chattered non-stop. Gilly let herself be pulled to the café, to be nudged into a chair, and then stared at the little white cup of espresso placed in front of her. Lifting it to her lips she savored the bitter taste. Her eyes focused with the jolt of caffeine and with a sigh she smiled at her roommates.

"Milan was wonderful. A beautiful city and Maxime, well Maxime was beyond belief—gallant, attentive, loving—"

"Skip stopped by to see you this afternoon," Nicole blurted out. As Nicole intended, the news of Skip's visit snapped Gilly out of her trance or whatever she was suffering from.

"Skip? Here?"

"Yeah," Sheridan replied. "He said to tell you he was sorry he missed you but that your tip, or whatever you told him, paid off and they arrested the woman. He said to thank you."

"Here?" Gilly, her brows scrunched, looked from one to the other.

"Well, he evidently was traveling with a detective from Seattle. The arrest took place in Monaco. He left here this afternoon to catch a flight back to Seattle with the detective." Nicole looked at Sheridan and back to Gilly's stricken face. They definitely had her full attention.

Gilly shook her head. Skip was in Monaco at the same moment she and Maxime were in Monaco … at the same time—

"Gilly, Sheridan and I have something else we have to tell you."

"What? About Skip?"

"No, it's about Maxime. Maxime Beaumont."

Gilly looked at her friends. Something was wrong. Very wrong. It was written all over their faces. She suddenly didn't want to hear. She wanted to be back in Milan, back with Maxime. "Did something happen to Skip?"

"No, not Skip. Maxime. Gilly…" Nicole looked to Sheridan for help.

Sheridan held Nicole's hand, leaned forward gripping Gilly's fingers with her other hand. "Gilly, Maxime is married."

Gilly raised her eyes to Sheridan, then to Nicole. She pulled her hand free from Sheridan's grip.

"He can't be. I don't know who told you such a thing, but they're mistaken. There are many Beaumont's in Paris, in France. I thought you were my friends. What were you doing? Sneaking around asking questions? Embarrassing Maxime?"

"There's no mistake," Nicole whispered.

Gilly's face contorted in pain, she searched for something in the eyes of roommates to confirm what they were saying was a lie told to them by some jealous woman. A joke. A horrible joke. But she saw nothing in Nicole's or Sheridan's facial expression denying their words.

Gilly jumped up, ran out to the sidewalk, ran down the street, arms wrapped around her body. She stopped abruptly, Sheridan and Nicole running up along side of her. Gilly's face was calm but her breathing was labored. She pulled her spine straight as she whirled to her friends. "He must be separated. There's no ring on his finger. He must be going through a divorce. A nasty divorce. You must have seen it in the newspaper. The gossip columns." She said the words through tight lips. "He didn't tell me because he's trying to shield me from what must be an awful time in his life."

There. That was it. That was the explanation. Of course, he didn't tell me. Gilly looked with narrowed eyes at the street lamp's sharp shadows.

"I have to unpack. Tomorrow is going to be a hectic day. The buyer told me she wanted my help in describing the details of the swatches she brought back."

Gilly turned and clipped along back to the apartment. At the front door, she paused. "I know you meant well. But there has to be an explanation. I know Maxime cares about me. When I have dinner with him on Friday I'll ask him. He'll clear up the misunderstanding. You'll see."

Chapter 14

Gilly inhaled a controlled, deep, breath slowly putting one foot in front of the other as she entered the familiar dimly lit restaurant. The musician sat at the piano playing a mournful love song, looked at her in recognition and smiled. She spotted Maxime sitting at a corner table in the back. Their table. Seeing her he stood and extended his hand magnetically pulling her to him.

Heads turned as the beautiful redhead in a black slender dress, her black strappy heels clicking on the tile floor, walked to the handsome man waiting for her. He kissed her as he helped her into her seat. What those who followed her entrance didn't see was that she turned her head slightly so his kiss was placed on her cheek and not her lips.

"I ordered champagne. I hope that's all right with you?" Maxime asked a hint of puzzlement in his eyes.

"Yes, fine."

"I've missed you, Gillianne. Only a few days ... forever." Maxime raised her hand to his lips but she pulled away. "What's wrong, my little bird? You're face is full of sadness."

"You're married?"

The piano music eddied through the intimate restaurant, each table cloaked in candlelight. A small number of tables remained in solitary, quietly waiting for patrons to bring them life.

The waiter poured the champagne.

Maxime quickly ordered their dinner.

The waiter left.

"Yes, I'm married," Maxime said slowly watching her expression. After a pause he continued. "We live apart. Most of the time."

"Why didn't you tell me?"

"I was afraid."

"Afraid?"

"Afraid you wouldn't share a drink with me. Then afraid you wouldn't share dinner with me. That I wouldn't hear the gaiety in your voice as you talked about your world of fashion. A world that brings passion to your voice. Then I wanted to bring that same passion to me."

Gilly's eyes misted, a single tear bridged the edge of her eye and dissolved on her cheek.

"Would you have seen me?" Maxime asked, dabbing her cheek gently with the soft white silk of his handkerchief.

"No."

"I thought not. I wanted you to know me before I told you. I was going to tell you while we were in Milan, but I didn't want to spoil our time together, our precious time alone. So I thought when we returned to Paris. Tonight. Can you understand? Can you forgive me for waiting, for wanting you?"

"I want to … but … I don't know … I …"

"Please, think about Milan … Monaco. Think about us. Sip your champagne and think about us. Give us a little time. Then if you must, you will return to Seattle … and that will be the end … if that is what you wish. Can you do that?"

"Yes, I can do that."

Chapter 15

End of July and Paris was experiencing a heat wave. It was Saturday afternoon and Parisians as well as tourists strolled along the banks of the Seine, marveling at the beauty of the river that cut through the city. Gilly sat alone on a bench under a shade tree staring at the sparkling water of the river as it rippled by. Dressed in white shorts and shirt, knotted at the waist, she felt a slight breeze cooling her skin.

A few gazed at the pretty redhead as they passed but none made eye contact. Gilly pulled her knees to her chest resting her bare feet on the bench, jeweled sandals laid on the grass beside her.

The Friday-night dinners with Maxime were becoming more and more strained since he admitted to her that he was married. She hadn't quizzed him further—waiting for him to tell her he was free, or soon would be. Five weeks had passed. He'd said nothing. She wondered about his family. Once, he had volunteered there were no children involved but what about his parents? Now that she thought about it, until she asked him if he was married, he'd never mentioned anything about his family, or friends for that matter. All he'd said was that he was a lawyer in a firm founded by his grandfather and that was when she first met him. Was he just concerned about a scandal or was he ashamed of her?

A couple strolled by—his arm around her shoulders, her arms around his waist. They paused. Kissed. Lovers.

Gilly looked away and reached into her pocket for her cell.

"Maria, hi. It's Gilly."

"Well, it's about time you called, girl friend. I miss you. How's everything in Paris? Learning a lot?"

"Yes. How are you, Hawk, the casino?"

"Wow. Let's see. Hawk passed his bar exam with flying colors. Now he's up to his eyeballs negotiating with the gaming commission on plans to expand the casino and resort. I'm fine. No, I'm better than fine. Oh, Gilly, I miss our chats. I think Hawk is going to pop the question. You know the big one?"

"That's wonderful, Maria."

"You don't sound good. Are you sure you're okay?"

"Just tired." Gilly felt a tightness grip her chest. "No, it's more than that, Maria. I feel like I've lost my way."

"Hey, maybe it's time to come home."

"That's just it. I've been thinking of staying in Paris, but I'm torn ... not sure. I'll be finished in another three months with the internships that my employment agent arranged. I've been offered a position in one of the companies—contributing to their designs. Then there's the modeling. I make good money, but that's not what I want to do. I don't like the model's life, *and* I don't want to design for someone else. Will you do me a favor?"

"Name it. You know I'll do whatever I can."

"Do you remember that loft? The one in the city?"

"The one you and I discussed about renting? You were going to use your savings—rent the space and start your line. That dream?"

"Yes, that one." Gilly leaned over, picked a blade of grass and looked out at a sightseeing boat slowly making its way down the river. Passengers out on the decks taking pictures of the buildings, statues, and other points of interest the guide was pointing out.

"I remember it was a nice spot. We thought it would be central to meeting the buyers who were going to beat down our doors for your designs." Maria giggled. "I hope you're still thinking of starting your own label. Of course you could always set up shop in your grandfather's guesthouse, Hansville. You'd be closer to me—I sure would like that."

"Maria, I've been dating."

"Oh oh. Does Skip know?"

"He may. He stopped by my apartment when I was out of town. He was on his way back from Monaco, through Paris. I didn't know he was in the area."

"Oh, Gilly, Skip had a big story in the Times. Ran exclusive under his byline ... it read like a novel. And now that you mention it, they did catch the woman in Monaco. I didn't put Monaco and Paris together. If he knows you're dating then that may be why he looks so miserable."

"Why do you say that? Did you see him?"

"Yes. Hawk and I stopped for a drink, you know our favorite watering hole on the waterfront … while we waited for the ferry. He was sitting at the bar and we asked him to join us. He asked about you and, when I said I hadn't heard from you lately, he made a comment like, 'maybe neither one of us will ever see her again.' Hawk and I talked about him. It wasn't like Skip. He's always been so intense, eager, loving what he was doing … loving life. Have you spoken to him?"

"Once. I called to tell him I was sure I saw the woman who disappeared, Mrs. Wellington, in one of the fitting rooms where I was modeling. He told my roommates that my tip had enabled the police to find and arrest her."

"Maybe your roommates told him about your dating. Are the Frenchmen as romantic as they say?"

"I'm afraid so," Gilly whispered.

"Gilly, I can't hear you. I don't like the way you sound."

"I'm fine, really. You have my cell. Let me know about that rental, and, Maria…"

"Yes."

"I miss you, too."

"Gilly, talk to me. What's the matter?"

"I will … not now. It's complicated."

Chapter 16

Seattle

Hot and humid and very sticky—typical Seattle weather for the beginning of August except today there was no rain in sight. Men walked in and out of office buildings with their jacket hung on a finger over their shoulder, visible rings of perspiration staining their shirts. Women wore sundresses, a jacket always handy on an office wall peg when they returned to their frigid air-conditioned offices.

Skip, sweat staining his blue short-sleeved shirt, tie askew, sat at his desk oblivious to the heat. The AC in the newsroom was on the fritz and only coughed up an occasional hunk of cool air. Maintenance promised to have the dreaded unit fixed by the end of the day. So the reporters had to suck it up and tough it out.

Skip let out a sigh. Another miserable Friday. Another miserable weekend. He sat tapping his pen on the blank yellow pad lying in front of him.

"Hey, Skipper, ready to go for our TGIF beer?"

Our TGIF beer. Where the hell did she come up with that? Twice, maybe three times, didn't equate to *our* in his mind. He turned on the little wheels of his squeaky chair to face her.

Diane. No, the beautiful Diane stood in the opening to his cubicle. Any other male in the newsroom would have killed to hear her say those words. Her face was flushed, eager to get him away from prying eyes. She was wearing a dress. A low cut black-halter dress with tiny pearl buttons all the way down the front, and a sweater draped over her shoulders.

Friday. Their *routine*, according to Diane, Friday after-work beer had just seemed to happen. Come on, stupid, he thought. Get your ass in gear and join the lady. *She* wants to be with you so snap out of it. No red hair? Who cares. He grabbed his blazer, straightened his tie, and pasted a smile on his face.

"You bet I'm ready. And, Miss Diane, if you're a good girl and agree to my offer, after the beer we'll grab some takeout and have dinner at my place. Sound okay?"

"Oooh, moving right along aren't we. How about we skip the beer thingy, pick up a bottle of wine and whatever, and go straight to your house?"

"Fine with me. Chinese okay?"

"You bet."

"And, my wine rack is ready to be plucked so one stop at Kung Fu Charlie's will provide everything else. Want to come with me or follow in your car?"

"Tonight I'll follow." She gave him a wink as he slapped a piece of paper into the palm of her outstretched hand with directions to his apartment just in case they got separated in traffic. No way in hell will we get separated tonight, she thought.

Thirty minutes later they were laughing over goblets of red wine as they sat on the floor leaning back against his couch eating egg foo yung, pork fried rice, and steamed broccoli with cashews. Dinner was casual, easy conversation swapping newsroom gossip and stories of other reporter's screw-ups.

Agatha pushed her bulky body between them and into his face as he was about to open his fortune cookie. Her leash was hanging out of both sides of her jaw.

"Knock it off, Aggie."

"Oh, does someone with four large paws planted in four different directions and wagging a stubby tail want to go out?" Diane said laughing.

"Looks like it." Skip pulled Diane to her feet and she took a chance inviting his lips to hers as she leaned again his chest. He looked into her very warm brown eyes and accepted the invitation. It felt nice, and he lingered on her plump pink lips. He pulled back slowly Aggie whining at his feet. "I think Miss Agatha wants to go for that walk now."

The night air hadn't cooled a bit, nor had the result of their embrace. Returning to the apartment Agatha fell fast asleep on her pillow and Skip slid a Neil Diamond CD in the player.

Shoes kicked off, Skip's blazer and tie cast aside on the chair, and sitting side-by-side on the black leather couch with another glass of wine, they chatted about her world as editor of the women's society pages. With the last drop of wine, Diane picked up their empty plates on the coffee table and Skip dumped the barren cartons into the garbage.

Returning from the kitchen, Diane brushed against him. "This is nice Skip. I'd never thought of having an apartment in the city—too noisy and too close to work. But at night the lights seem to have a calming effect and with the music you don't hear the street sounds."

Putting his hand on her shoulder he turned her to him, kissed her firmly, then held her close. She couldn't see that his eyes were closed but she could feel his heart race.

Pulling back she skimmed her fingers over the fuzz on his head pulling him to her open mouth. "Kiss me again, Skipper. That was good."

He pulled her down on the couch, his hands skimming her curves, his lips kissing her face, her neck. She unbuttoned the top three buttons of her dress and he moaned as his lips wandered down from her neck to her breast. "So long. Way to long."

Her blood was rushing. Pulse rapid. "Why, Skipper, I didn't know you felt that way. I—"

Skip opened his eyes, looked at her flushed face … waiting … wanting him.

Carefully he slid her to the floor so he could sit up.

"I'm sorry, Diane. This was a mistake. I didn't mean to—"

"Mean to? I hoped you would. Unless you don't want to—"

Skip stood, rubbed his hands over his head, started pacing. What the hell is the matter with you, he thought. It's Friday and this beautiful woman wants you to make love to her. And you put on the brakes just because she doesn't have green eyes? "God, what am I doing?"

"Well, I'm not sure what you're doing," Diane said, standing while buttoning her dress. "You're either very tired, a monk, or thinking about an old girl friend. Either way, I think it best if I go."

"I'm sorry, Diane."

"Don't be sorry, I just hope you figure out what you want."

"I'll walk you to your car."

"Thank you."

Skip snapped on Agatha's leash and he walked Diane and his dog to the elevator. Neither said another word. She triggered the locks on her car, slid in and opened the window.

"If you decide you want to see me, ME, let me know," she said with a little smile and drove off leaving the man standing on the curb with his dog.

Chapter 17

Thirty-year-old Edward Churchill limped slowly around his Seattle hotel room. The wrecking crew passed the hotel by during the years of the city's revitalization leading up to the 1962 World's Fair. The year the Space Needle was opened for business.

A sharp pain in Edward's foot forced him to flop down on the musty bedspread. Even though Edward's mother continued to fund his bank account, the fleabag hotel was all Edward felt he could afford.

He had to save his money for his yet undetermined revenge against Gillianne Wilder. So what if he had grabbed her by the throat. He had fled to Mexico after his encounter with the redhead because she sicced the law on him. It was there he spent the last year undergoing three botched operations to fuse his ankle, leaving him in pain—sometimes terrible, other times bearable, depending on the vagaries of the weather. The pain a constant reminder of how much he hated the woman. The police tired of searching for him, or so he was told by his grandmother, so he returned to the States. He traveled straight to Seattle to settle his score with the bitch.

Edward had been a designer at a prestigious fashion house in New York City where, because of Ms. Wilder, he lost his job. Fired. No one would hire him after that. No one believed in him after that except his mother and his grandmother. He had them both fooled, but not his Wall Street, stock-market-genius father.

His grandmother, Helen Churchill, from the hick town Port Gamble, near another hick town, Hansville, had asked Ms. Wilder to design a gown for her to wear to a posh wedding to be held in New York. Because of his grandmother he came to Washington to meet the designer from the sticks. He saw her all right. Visited her and took pictures of her sketches while she fixed him coffee, designs he later incorporated into his designs for a marketing catalog printed by his company. He didn't see any harm in *copying* her designs. She was a nobody, her work barely passable. Gilly accused him of stealing her designs. He preferred to think of it as borrowing ideas and making them better.

Helen Churchill had shown the catalog to Ms. Wilder one day. Of course she recognized her designs and immediately talked to her friend Hawk Jackson—an Indian studying to be a lawyer for his tribe operating a casino a few miles south of Hansville.

Hawk had sent him a letter warning him to never steal Ms. Wilder's designs again. The jerk-lawyer mailed a copy to Edward's boss who fired him on the spot saying he hadn't had an original idea for years. Good riddance.

Edward did admit to himself that he had made one mistake. He shouldn't have visited the bitch in Hansville threatening to kill her for getting him fired. He should have waited until he was sober, but he had to see her. He was always drinking anyway. He yelled at her. She yelled back. He had lunged at her, placing his hands around her throat. Then the bitch's grandfather came storming out of the patio door with a shotgun aimed right him. He yelled at Edward, too. He fired the gun while Edward was trying to escape on his motorcycle, hitting him in the foot. Edward didn't see a doctor until the pain got so bad he had to seek help.

No, Edward was not about to let Gillianne Wilder rise in the fashion world. Trouble was he couldn't find her.

Well, it was time he did something and he knew just how to go about it. His grandmother, Helen Churchill, believed Gillianne walked on water. And, his grandmother lived in Port Gamble, a mere twenty minutes away from Hansville, where the Wilder family seemed to be staying with Gillianne's grandfather, the wretched old man who shot him.

It was time to seek revenge for the pain they had caused him.

"Hello, Grandmother."

"Edward, is that really you?"

"Yes, it is. Your favorite grandson."

"My only grandson. Where are you?"

"Doesn't matter where I am. I'm trying to find Gillianne Wilder."

"Edward, you stay away from that girl. You're lucky the police didn't put you in jail after what you did. My gracious, stealing Gilly's designs. They told me all about it."

"Lies, Grandmother. Did you know that her grandfather shot me. Nearly killed me."

"I've asked your father if he knew where you were. He didn't know or didn't want to tell me. And, of course I wouldn't ask your mother. We don't exactly see eye-to-eye. Are you all right?"

Good old dad, he thought. He never offered to help me. If it wasn't for mom, I'd be out on the street but as long as she feeds money into my account I can get by. No more having to meet those silly seasonal fashion deadlines with more, always more, and more designs for the next collection. That old man really did me a favor. I didn't like the fashion business anyway. They were always hounding me for another sketch. Stupid people.

"No. I told you the old geezer shot me. I'm always in pain but I thought I'd tell Gillianne that I forgive her. Don't want bad blood between us." Bad blood? He mused. I'd like to see her feel the pain I live with every day. Nothing fatal just a little fear of what might happen next time and the next.

"She's in Paris working at some of the fashion houses. Saw her mother just the other day. Anne hoped her daughter would come home in another month, but she wasn't sure."

"Thanks, Grandmother. You wouldn't happen to have her address would you?"

"Wait, I just might have it. Got it from her mother a couple of months ago. Wrote to ask her if she had been to the Louvre. Your grandfather and I went there once—one of the world's largest museums you know. Yes, here it is. Are you ready?"

"Oh, yes, I'm ready." Edward wrote down the address, thanked his grandmother for her help and hung up.

Edward hopped around the thread-bare carpet. Oh, this was going to be fun. He had already prepared a watch-sized jewelry box for his first message to her after the long hiatus—a red heart with a steel spike piercing the satin.

Since leaving her in front of her grandfather's guesthouse, wiping blood from her lip where he hit her, he changed his hair. Shaved it off. He used to gel the thick black locks into spikes on the top of his head—fashionable for young men in New York City. In fact, Gilly nicknamed him *Spiky*. He didn't like it at first, then thought better of it. Rather fit his personality—ill tempered, aggressive, violent—his attitude toward Ms. Wilder.

~ ~ ~

Paris

It was late when Gilly returned to the apartment—a full day listening to the marketing staff explaining the upcoming campaign to the designer on how they were going to position next spring's collection. She threw her bag on the floor and headed to the bathroom to take a shower. Her roommates would be home any minute and she wanted a shower while the water was still steamy hot.

Padding on wet feet, a white bathrobe and towel wrapped around freshly washed hair, she headed to the refrigerator and a cold drink. Nicole and Sheridan bolted in the door chattering about their hard day and handed a small box wrapped in brown paper to Gilly.

"Thanks, I was too tired to check …"

"What's the matter, Gilly. Did you see a ghost?" Nicole giggled.

There was no return address. Postmarked Seattle.

Gilly's fingers trembled as she tore away the brown paper.

"Hey, come on. Maybe there's a piece of jewelry inside," Sheridan said looking at Gilly's white face.

Gilly lifted the top of the box and there it was—a red heart with a steel spike through it. She slowly lifted her right hand, feeling the tiny scar on her lip.

Nicole picked up the box from Gilly's hand and pulled out the card.

"Hi, bet you thought I'd forgotten you. Wrong.
I'll never forget you, BITCH! Spiky."

"Who's Spiky?" Nicole asked handing the box and card to Sheridan.

"A man from New York. He stole my designs and when I accused him he lunged at me. My grandfather heard us yelling, charged out of the house with a gun and shot at him. We found blood after he stormed away on his motorcycle so Gramps is pretty sure he hit him."

"You recognized the package. Knew what was inside," Sheridan said. "It's not a very nice note. I take it you've seen something like this before."

"Yes. Gramps threw a celebration dinner for me at the Space Needle when I won the State design competition. Midway through the party a waiter handed me a box just like this. Said a man asked him to give it to me."

"Was there a card like this one?" Nicole asked.

"Almost word for word. It's been over nine months. I thought that night at the Space Needle was him letting out his frustration. That he was over it. I guess not."

"Why the name Spiky? Sounds rather silly." Sheridan returned the card to the box.

"His hair. He used a lot of gel, pulling his hair into spikes. I called him Spiky."

"Postmarked Seattle. Are you afraid of him?" Sheridan asked.

Gilly again touched the scar on her lip. "He tried to strangle me."

Chapter 18

The steel spike penetrating the satin heart unnerved Gilly more than she let on. She felt off balance, vulnerable, tears springing up suddenly, and a feeling of nausea from the tension. Was he now in Paris?

Hurrying down the street to a last minute modeling assignment, her eyes scanned the faces of every man passing by. Spiky? She pulled up short at the window of a bakery watching the reflections of the people as they hurried to the corner. Was that man following her? No. She continued down the street at a slower pace, ruminating over the package wrapped in brown paper. Maybe she should call Skip. He knows about Spiky.

She entered the fitting room, smiled faintly at the seamstress, and undressed. Bending forward, her arms outstretched, the seamstress floated the gown of black silk and sequins over Gilly's head allowing it to fall into place over her bare skin and began nipping and tucking to fit her curves.

"I saw you talking with that Maxime Beaumont the other day," the seamstress said fidgeting with the bodice of the gown. "He's handsome that one. Stuck in a nasty marriage."

"Ouch."

"Sorry, mademoiselle. I swear your bust line has changed or the measurements I was given are wrong. There, that should do it. Off with you, they're waiting in the main salon."

Gilly stared at her reflection in the mirror, "your bust line has changed" ringing in her ears.

"Mademoiselle, go, go."

Gilly glided down the hall to the salon, apprehension suddenly gripping her body. *Your bust line has changed. Your bust line has changed.* Seven weeks had passed since she returned from Milan.

Lately she had skipped her morning coffee—she had no taste for it. Nerves, she thought. Nothing to worry about. Her period was only a little late.

"Ms. Wilder, please walk around once more, then turn slowly so madame can see the gown from all angles," the saleslady said.

Slowly performing the moves, Gilly made a half turn and smiled, her mind spinning.

It is possible, she thought. No, no. I'll check. That's what I'll do. Check. No need to worry for nothing. Check."

Dismissed from the salon, Gilly hurriedly dressed leaving the sequined gown in the seamstress's hands. Quickly walking down the street, she entered the first pharmacie she came to. Snatching a bottle of shampoo, a package of tissues and a pregnancy test kit, she paid the cashier. It was mid afternoon. Sheridan was modeling for a different designer but she wasn't sure about Nicole.

Entering the apartment Nicole was sitting in her shorts and T-shirt at the little table reading a magazine.

"You're home early," Nicole said glancing up and back to the magazine.

Gilly didn't reply. Dropping her large leather tote on the couch she hurried into the bathroom clutching the bag from the drugstore. Removing the test kit from the box, she quickly read the instructions: 3 minutes ... results in words ... pregnant ... not pregnant, 99% accurate.

Within minutes she left the bathroom and slumped down on the couch.

"Hey, what's the matter?" Nicole rushed to her friend. She knelt down in front of Gilly, and looked into her pasty-white face. Anxiety filled eyes.

Gilly handed her the blue and white tester.

"Pregnant."

Nicole looked at the meter and then back to Gilly and the tears streaming down her face.

"Now, you listen to me, Gillianne Wilder. Maxime's marriage is said to be all but over. You love him, and he obviously loves you. The way he's been meeting you—courting really. Tomorrow's Friday and you're meeting him for dinner? Right?"

Gilly nodded she was. Taking the tissue Nicole handed her she blotted at the tears on her cheeks.

Nicole grasped Gilly's arms and shook her gently. "You pull yourself together, put on your prettiest dress and be prepared to be wrapped in his arms. He's going to tell you he'll get the divorce as quickly as possible. It's going to work out. And, Gilly, what a little miracle you're holding. You're going to have a baby. Now, let me see a smile. Come on now." Nicole looked at her dear friend as Gilly's lips slowly drew into a tentative smile.

Blinking back the remaining tears, she rested her hand on her belly. Nicole covered Gilly's hand with her own then pulled Gilly to her feet wrapping her in her arms, rocking slowly from side to side.

Gilly nestled into Nicole's arms, laying her head on her shoulder.

"It's going to be all right, you'll see," Nicole whispered.

Chapter 19

The water beating down was warm and soothing as it sluiced over her body. Gilly held her face up to the showerhead massaging the shampoo thru her hair, enjoying the beat of the water washing the soap away, filling the air with a strawberry scent. Turning the water off she grabbed the white fluffy towel and tucked it around her body.

She smiled at her reflection as the steam receded from the mirror. Another two hours and she'd be with Maxime telling him of their baby in the soft glow of candlelight.

She pumped several dabs of the new body lotion Nicole had given her for this special evening. Letting the towel drop she stroked the lotion on her legs and arms, looking in the mirror gently adding some to her belly. It was hard to believe there was a tiny tiny person in there. The thought thrilled her—her mother was younger when she'd given birth to Gilly. I'll call mom tomorrow, she thought. Oh, she's going to be so excited.

Gilly finished dressing and shot a spritz of her favorite perfume in the air, leaned into the mist leaving a light scent around her bare shoulders. Her strapless black dress, nipped under her breasts, fell softly down over her hips to just above her knees, her feet in backless heels held by small straps crisscrossing over her red painted toes.

Gilly stood in front of the mirror, smoothed her dress, turned sideways—nothing showed ... yet. Her breasts were fuller but other than that her dress still fit. With a deep breath she left the bathroom and stood in front of Nicole and Sheridan. "How do I look?"

"Like a million bucks," Sheridan said. "The guy would be crazy to let you go. Champagne tonight?"

"Just a little."

"Here, would you like to wear my diamond earrings?" Nicole asked holding the sparkling gems out to Gilly.

"Oh, yes, they're beautiful, Nicole," she said replacing her gold hoops with the diamonds.

"Just remember, no matter what happens, Nicole and I will be waiting for you." Sheridan gave Gilly a quick hug. Nicole did the same whispering we love you in her ear.

"Wish me luck," Gilly said as she disappeared out the door.

Almost the end of August and the evening air was heavy with moisture. The summer heat seemed to overwhelm everyone on the streets, their steps lethargic. The disgruntled cab driver, sweat soaking the neckband of his T-shirt, grumbled about the heat.

Within minutes Gilly was entering the restaurant. She relaxed a little seeing Maxime sitting at their table. He stood and smiled at her his arm outstretched, grasping her hand, kissing each cheek in greeting.

The waiter instantly appeared at the table, popped the champagne cork, and filled their crystal flutes, the bubbles sparkling in the candlelight. Nestling the bottle in a bed of ice in the silver bucket he looked at Maxime, ready to take his dinner order. Maxime asked him to come back—they would wait to order. He turned to Gilly.

"Gillianne my sweet, you are more beautiful, more radiant tonight than ever. You must have had a good week since I saw you last."

"I missed you, Maxime."

"I missed you, too. Tell me what brings such sparkle to your eyes, and then I have something to tell you."

Oh, my God, maybe he's going to tell me he's getting his divorce sooner than he had believed possible. Nicole and Sheridan are right. Everything is going to be okay—her hand lying in her lap, the palm turned against her body. He's so handsome, so kind, so caring. So loving.

"You go first," Gilly said, running her fingers playfully over the tops of his knuckles holding his glass. She reached for her champagne and took a sip, her green eyes warm and bright as rare emeralds.

"All right." Maxime took several swallows of champagne waving off the waiter for a second time.

"I'm going to run for the Senate."

Gilly felt her heart seize. What did this mean?

"My wife and I are reconciling for the campaign. If I win she will remain by my side. If I lose we will separate again."

Gilly pulled her hand away. Burned. Panic raced through her veins, clutched at every pore of her body, her breasts rising and falling with each gulp of air.

"I'm afraid we won't be able to see each other very often. Of course, I will try to arrange seeing you the best I can. I hope you—"

Gilly, her legs feeling like tall grass bending in the wind, managed to stand, held the back of her chair for support, and looked down at her lover. "You hope I'll what? Understand?" she whispered.

Maxime reached for her hand. "Wait."

"Yes, I understand exactly what you're saying. Goodbye, Maxime."

Chapter 20

The roommates were watching their favorite television show when they heard the sound of a key being inserted into the front-door lock. Nicole and Sheridan looked at each other, the clock and back to each other. It was only ten o'clock. Was Gilly home so soon?

The door swung open. The girl who left the apartment two hours ago was not the girl who walked into the apartment. The person who stood before them, a take-out coffee in her hand, was a stone-faced woman—no girly smile, no twinkling eyes, no bounce in her step.

Sheridan reached for the remote and snapped off the TV. Gilly dropped her clutch on the small table beside a padded chair, then slowly lowered herself into the chair, crossed her legs, and sipped her coffee—all without moving her eyes from her roommates. Nicole and Sheridan ready to rush to her stopped in their tracks and returned to the couch, staring back at the woman. The eerie double blare of an ambulance passed the building. The sound faded and silence again filled the void.

Gilly's face remained expressionless.

"Maxime Beaumont is putting together his campaign to run for the Senate. He and his wife have reconciled their differences."

Taking off the diamond earrings, Gilley leaned forward and handed them to Nicole.

"What are you going to do?" Nicole whispered.

"I just spent the last hour at our café asking myself that very question."

"And?" Nicole asked, the diamond earrings clenched in her fist.

"I'm going to finish my two-week assignment with the fashion-house buyer. The designer and her team are making the final choices from the fabric swatches the buyer picked out in Milan. I want to be in on the decision-making process."

Gilly kicked off her heels, drew her legs up underneath her. "Then … I'm going home, rent a small studio in downtown Seattle and design my first collection under my label. And … seven and a half months from now I'll have this baby."

"Are you going to put the baby up for adoption? What about an abortion?" Sheridan asked.

"No. My baby was created from my love, my passion for its father. It is mine and it will be cherished as a gift of love." Gilly laid her hand on her belly. "A gift of love."

"What are you going to say when people ask you about the father?"

"The identity of the father will go with me to my grave, and I ask that you hold my secret dear to your hearts. I've started to formulate a story about the father and I'd like your thoughts."

"Tell us," Nicole said, scooting down on the floor, wrapping her arms around her legs and looking into Gilly's passionless face.

Gilly finished her coffee and set the empty cup on the table. She leaned her head back. Looked at the ceiling.

"I met a man in Paris. It was love at first sight. He's an agent for the French government and performs dangerous missions. Twice he was called away. I never knew where. He told me if he didn't return one day it was because he was killed. He is dead. No siblings, and his parents were killed in an automobile accident shortly after he was born. No family. No contacts."

The air conditioner kicked in, droning, as the three processed the story, the fabricated story, the lie.

"I guess that means you didn't tell Maxime about the baby?" Nicole said.

"He told me of his plans to run for the Senate before I had a chance. I did the only thing I could do. I said goodbye … left him … standing in the restaurant." She shifted in the chair and looked into their somber faces. "So, any suggestions, changes to my story? It's basically I met a man, fell in love, and he was killed in the service of his country. We were not married. The baby will be raised with the Wilder name."

"It sounds plausible I guess," Sheridan said. "Let's sleep on it. Tomorrow is Saturday. We'll have our usual breakfast at the café. Take a walk. If you still want to tell that story, then that's it."

"You two will be the only ones who know the truth. If anyone should ask, you say you were aware I had met a man and that he was killed. I never told you his name or anything about him. I kept everything private. Okay?"

"What about your family?" Nicole asked.

"I met a man, we fell in love, I became pregnant, and he was killed in the service of his country."

"And Skip?"

"I met a man, we fell in love, I became pregnant, and he was killed in the service of his country."

"I'll can't believe you're taking this so calmly." Nicole sat on her hands rocking back and forth.

"Calm? My world has changed forever. I was a stupid, naive girl with very poor judgment. She is no more. Maybe someday I'll let myself shed the tears behind the dam I've erected inside me … but not now. If I let it burst now … I … I … well, I can't allow those dark thoughts to enter my head."

"You're a brave woman, Gillianne," Sheridan said. "I'll ask you if this is what you want tomorrow. If it is, your secret will be safe with me."

"That goes for me, too," Nicole said.

"One last thing. If anyone questions you about Maxime, all you know is that we had dinner a few times, nothing more. After all he *is* a married man."

Chapter 21

The cab pulled down the street from the apartment, rounded the corner giving Gilly one last glimpse of the little café where she, Nicole, and Sheridan had spent so many hours over espressos laughing, planning, pooling what they learned on any given day at the feet of a designer's staff member, or the factories where her staff assembled samples, then to the cutting rooms, the sewing rooms, and then the final products delivered around the world.

Gilly waved to Tony as they passed. He saluted her. Nicole, Sheridan and Gabby sitting in the back seat remained quiet with their thoughts. Gilly, sitting in front alongside the driver, stared out the window as the streets of Paris rolled by. The Louvre, the Seine, monuments, cafes their patrons chatting—hands punctuating conversations. Paris. The city she came to love, a city where she briefly thought she might live, and now she was leaving. She doubted she'd ever be back.

Maxime. What if she bumped into him. She could never take that chance. That man ... sitting outside at the café ... Maxime? She turned her head as the cab passed. Letting out a sigh ... of course, it wasn't him. She felt her eyes mist, blinked away the mist quickly. She couldn't let one tear escape because she didn't know how many more might follow.

The cab picked up speed—flower stands, bright awnings, cafes always the cafes, fountains spewing water into the sunlight and gathering in sparkling pools at their base.

This ride to the airport so different than the one six months earlier— she and Gabby, giddy, laughing, carefree. Passing *The House of Chanel* Gabby slipped her hand into Nicole's. Electric. Their unspoken thoughts were shared nonetheless—one day they would be in a cab leaving Paris for Seattle. The House of Gillianne was going to be known worldwide. Gilly was a rising designer. More than once in the past few months her designs had been incorporated into the house's collection.

Sheridan was looking out her side window and didn't see Gabby grip Nicole's hand. She didn't share the optimism of the pair. In her mind Gilly was running home, running away, defeated and pregnant. No, Sheridan had to keep looking for an opportunity to make it big.

The cab drew up to the American Airlines terminal.

Gilly stepped out of the cab with her friends. The roommates and her agent insisted on seeing her safely off for her return flight to Seattle. They hustled up to the baggage check in. Sheridan rolled her large suitcase, Gabby another medium-sized suitcase, and Nicole the carry-on. Gilly had already shipped most of her stuff, stuff she bought for her family and Maria.

With her boarding pass in hand, Gilly made a quick call to Maria letting her know she would call from JFK for the second leg of her trip, thanking her again for her offer to meet her in Seattle.

"Do you have time for a quick coffee?" Nicole asked.

"I think not. My stomach is a little on edge … excitement and all I guess. There is one thing I want to float out to you," she said glancing from one to the other. "If … no, not if, when I start my business I'll be calling to see if any of you would like to help me. It would be rough at first and slim pay, but I will be able to offer you a place to stay even if it's at my grandfather's," she said smiling.

Gabby and Nicole answered at the same time. "Yes." They looked at each other and giggled. "I guess what we're trying to say," Gabby offered, "Is that we'd both be interested. Having never been to the States, and to have a chance at putting some of what we've learned to work," again they giggled. "It would be beyond wonderful."

"Exactly," Nicole said. "I guess you're thinking of starting in Seattle?"

"Yes." Gilly looked at Sheridan.

"I have more to do here, but promise you'll call when you open up shop in New York." Sheridan smiled at Gilly. "What about … you know … the baby?"

"The baby adds another word to my bio—mother. My mother took me to a tearoom where she was a hostess when I was a baby."

Gilly looked at her watch and then back at her friends, hugging each in turn. "You've been terrific. I'm going to miss you."

"Hey, no tears, young lady." Gabby retrieved a tissue from her bag and handed it to Gilly. "And, you'd better let us know how everything is going and not just occasionally. I'm thinking at least once a week."

"Yeah, at least," Nicole said hugging Gilly one last time.

"We mean *everything*." Sheridan said.

An hour later the jet taxied down the runway. Gilly strained at her seatbelt, forehead pressed to the plane's window. Six months. She had been in Paris six months. She came as girl and was leaving a woman carrying a treasure that would forever tie her to the beautiful city. She had learned a lot about the fashion industry but more to the point, she had learned about life … what love was and what it wasn't.

Chapter 22

Seattle

The silver plane circled, banked, and began its descent into SeaTac Airport. Puget Sound, the piers and skyscrapers of Seattle, and the Space Needle spread out below.

Home.

Deplaning, pulling her small rolling case, a large tote over her shoulder, Gilly trotted along with the crowd to Baggage Claim.

Spotting Gilly, Maria and Hawk waved from the top of the escalator. She didn't see them at first, her head down watching the moving metal stair treads so she didn't fall. She was a little apprehensive about coming home and had decided not to say anything about her pregnancy to her friend until after she told her parents.

The minute she saw Maria waving frantically to get her attention, relief spread through her body. Her best friend stood at the top of the stairs, her arms open wide in greeting. Gilly leaned into her and hugged back trying to stem the tears but a few escaped. Hawk immediately pulled his handkerchief from his pocket and handed it Gilly.

"I don't know what's the matter with me. It's so incredibly wonderful to see you both."

"Come on let's get your luggage. I brought reinforcements." Maria nodded at Hawk. He grabbed the handle of her suitcase and Maria laughed tucking her arm through Gilly's and at the same time squeezing Hawk's free hand. She threw him a quick glance. Something was wrong with Gilly as she had all but collapsed in Maria's arms. She didn't know what it was and probably wouldn't find out until they got together tomorrow. Maria fully intended to drop by the Wilder's Hansville home by lunchtime and steal Gilly away.

The friends chatted all the way to the Seattle ferry terminal, and never stopped as they crossed Puget Sound. Maria and Hawk peppered her with questions about Paris: the weather, the food, the cafes, and the people. They were both careful not to ask anything personal sensing immediately *personal* was out of bounds after Gilly waved off their first inquiries about her roommates and, of course, the man Gilly had mentioned during a few of their telephone conversations.

Two hours later, Hawk turned down the Wilder's driveway honking the horn as he pulled to a stop.

Gramps was the first out of the house followed by Anne and Will, Gilly's mom and dad. Hawk retrieved the luggage scooting around the welcoming committee, depositing the cases on the patio and trotted back to Maria. Maria stood beside him smiling at the family reunion. So loving, she thought. I have a feeling she's going to need it.

Anne invited Maria and Hawk in for a cup of coffee, but they begged off. They had Gilly for a couple of hours and now it was her family's turn. Gilly hugged Hawk and then Maria, thanking them for picking her up and confirmed a lunch date tomorrow with Maria.

Anne walked in the house, her arm around her daughter, followed on their heels by Will and Gramps.

Settling at the kitchen table *again*, Gilly wondered if the past six months had really happened. Was she ever in Paris?

"Will, I think this calls for a bottle of champagne," Anne said sitting next to Gilly at the table.

Gilly looked up sharply but decided not to refuse. A sip would be okay. Until …

Will retrieved a bottle from the refrigerator chilling for the occasion, popped the cork, and poured the bubbly into the goblets Anne had set out.

"Here's to Gillianne's safe return home. Where you belong I might add," her dad said.

"You look tired, sugar. How many hours since you left Paris?" Gramps asked.

"With the plane changes … over fourteen hours."

"Your dad and I are back at home in Port Gamble," Anne said smiling at her husband.

"I was lucky and landed a job again over the winter at Port Townsend—renovating an existing condo complex," Will said, taking a sip of champagne.

"Good for you, Dad."

Gilly gazed out the big picture window at the sparkling waters of the sound. A tanker headed north, low in the water with a load of cargo picked up at one of the Seattle piers. Back in the arms of her family she wondered how she could have been so stupid. She was suddenly filled with hatred for Maxime.

"I have something to tell you," Gilly said staring out the window.

Anne patted her daughter's hand. "Honey, you don't have to tell us about your time in Paris now. Why don't—"

Turning, looking into her mother's face, so like her own, "I have to tell you now. I'm pregnant."

Anne's hand dropped to her lap, a gasp of air escaping her mouth.

Will set his glass down on the table. "What?" he asked in a hissed whisper.

"Let her speak, son," Gramps said. "Tell us what happened, child."

"I met a man, a Frenchman, shortly after I arrived in Paris. The only thing I can say, or have the strength to say right now, is that he was an agent for the French government. We fell in love at first sight."

"Gilly, you said he *was* an agent," Anne said. "What does he do now? Is he coming to be with you in Seattle?"

"He's dead."

"Oh, Gilly," Anne grasped her daughter's hand, held it to her cheek, eyes closed. "My poor girl."

"How?" Will asked his voice gruff, eyes narrowed.

"When I inquired, all they would say is that he was killed in action. They only told me that much because he had no family. I was the only one to inquire."

"How far along are you?" Will asked squinting at his daughter.

"Almost three months. Sometime late March. Mom, I'd like to make an appointment with your doctor or whomever you suggest."

"You haven't been to a doctor?"

"No. But there's no doubt."

"We'll go home and I'll call first thing in the morning for you."

"Okay, but I'm going to stay here with Gramps. Maria is coming over in the morning. I want to see what she thinks of my plans."

"Your plans? I trust this revelation means you're giving up that cockamamie idea of becoming a fashion designer," Will said knocking back his drink.

Her father's face had hardened as she told them she was pregnant. She knew he wasn't going to like what she was planning to do. She was sorry for that, but she had to keep moving, moving forward, keep her dream in front of her to create a life for herself and her baby.

Chapter 23

The guesthouse was as Gilly had left it six months prior—eight-foot table in the center of the little living room, three sewing machines on the table—hers, her mom's, Maria's—two mannequins—Patty and Suzy—at one end and a green plastic garden chair at the other.

Hearing Maria's car turn into the driveway, she stepped out into the brilliant September sunshine feeling it a good omen on her first day home. A big grin spread across her face—both girls wore their signature jeans, white T-shirt and sweater knotted around their shoulders. Gilly grasped Maria's hand pulling her into the guesthouse and the two best friends hugged each other. Gilly turned away, quickly blotting a tear.

"No place to sit in here," she said regaining her composure. "There's coffee on the counter. Help yourself and then I guess we might as well make ourselves comfortable on the bunk beds. I checked this morning and they're still there."

"Like old times ... before you left. I can just see you and I and your mom sewing like crazy on those machines trying to finish in time for the State competition—which you won, girl friend." Giggling, Maria poured a cup of coffee, and Gilly picked up the glass of milk. The girls moved to the little bedroom and settled on the lower bunk leaning against pillows shoved against the wall. So much to share ... but where to start.

"Gilly, I know you haven't told me everything. I can see it on your face. You're holding back."

"Okay, but you first. When you and Hawk picked me up yesterday you seemed close—so much in love."

"Oh, we are. He's wonderful. Now that he's passed the bar, he's replaced the tribe's part-time lawyer. The casino is going great guns. The whole resort is growing."

"And the resort's spa? Are you still working your magic?" Gilly asked, wrapping her arms around her knees, as she took a sip of milk.

"Still there and still loving the interaction with the guests. Hawk and I have been making some long-range plans. He wants to handle more than just the reservation's needs. He's looking to open an office in Seattle. But the big news," Maria said scrunching around to face Gilly, "We're talking about getting married in December—before Christmas. Can you believe it? I'm going to marry that handsome Indian."

"Oh, Maria, that's wonderful." Gilly grasped and squeezed her friend's hand with delight. "But what does that mean about the spa? Will you still manage it? Where will you live—the reservation, Seattle?"

"We're not sure. I love the spa, don't get me wrong, but I do miss being in the fashion industry. I loved working with you. Getting ready for the competition was so much fun."

Gilly arched her brows.

"Oh, I know it was a lot of work, but I loved it." Maria stared down into her coffee, and then looked up. "I've been waiting for you to come back I guess … waiting to hear what you're planning."

"Now that's what I call a segue. Hey, it's a beautiful day. How about we take a walk on the beach? I have so much to tell you and, with what you've just said, my mind is spinning with possibilities."

"Sounds good. Let's go."

The girls trotted to the front of the house, down over the bank on the rickety weather-beaten stairs to the deck and the beach below. The tide was out leaving an expanse of beach but they kept their shoes on for protection against the sharp stones.

Gilly stooped to pick up a tiny conch shell. Caressing it with her finger she thought about the little person growing inside of her. With her friend next to her, she felt a stirring of warmth for the first time since she had confirmed she was pregnant. Without looking up she announced, "Maria, I'm going to have a baby."

Maria stopped walking, closed her eyes. She knew Gilly was holding something back but having a baby was not what she expected. Opening her eyes wide, she reached for Gilly's arm. "Gilly, are you kidding me?"

"It's true." How wonderful it felt to be with her best friend. They had been through a lot together since that fateful day they met sitting side-by-side in the Fashion Academy auditorium—their first day of school. Looking into Maria's big brown eyes shining back at her—how much she loved her.

"Well, where is this man? Is it the Frenchman you mentioned on the phone?"

Confused for a moment—snapping back to reality, Gilly looked to the sky, the clouds scuttling across the sound. "Yes. But … he's dead."

"Dead?" The air suddenly sucked out of her hearing the fatal word, Mari's demeanor instantly changed from gaiety to dread.

"Yes. He worked for the government. He was killed. No family."

"That's awful. How can you be so composed?"

"I've accepted it. He never knew about the baby. He died shortly after I conceived. I haven't seen a doctor yet, but I figure it will be born sometime in late March … early April."

"Oh, my God. What are you going to do?" Maria, could only imagine what Gilly must be going through. But she was looking at a woman who was calm, almost serene. One whose world you would never guess was in turmoil.

"Do? I'm going to move forward. Build a life for us."

"Does Skip know?" Maria whispered. Heads down, the girls continued to walk along the beach like robots, much slower now caught in their own thoughts about the situation, pulling them closer, leaning on each other, giving, receiving support.

Gilly was startled by the question.

"Skip? Heavens, no. And if for some reason you see him, please don't say anything. It will be obvious soon. I told my family yesterday, and I certainly understand you'll share my condition with Hawk. As for anyone else, well, I'll deal with the questions as they come up. Skip? Maria, there's no room in my life for a man. Not now. Never again."

"Oh, Gilly, don't say that. Skip cares for you. The last time I saw him he looked terrible. I guess he stopped to see you but you were out of the city."

Gilly's chest tightened. She couldn't think about those days in Milan. No. Stop! Say something. Anything.

"Maria, I called a realtor this morning about an apartment in downtown Seattle. Checking on rents. It's much too expensive right now."

Maria gaped at her friend. "You didn't just change the subject, you turned it upside down, and now you're telling me you called a realtor. Whatever for?"

"Why?" She squeezed Maria's hand, turned to her with a grin, her green eyes regaining some of their sparkle. "To start my business, silly. I plan to launch my label with a five-piece collection—The Career Woman, Fashions by Gillianne Wilder. Will you help me? Not in Seattle. Not yet anyway. Here in the guesthouse … *then* Seattle after the baby is born."

Maria's breath escaped her lips. "Whew, tell me more." She spotted two logs, the tips touching at the top spreading out at the base. "Let's sit over there. You've rendered my legs to putty."

They sat on the logs facing each other, Gilly's excitement erupting as she spoke non-stop of her thoughts, schemes and dreams. It felt so good to jump on the merry-go-round, reach for the brass ring, conquering the world with Maria beside her.

"First off—money. I have fifteen thousand left from winning the competition. I didn't dip into that little nest egg while in Paris. In fact I added to it with modeling jobs. Which means I still don't have near enough money to set up a studio in Seattle, not yet anyway. Plus, I'll pay you as I ramp up."

Maria shook her head. "You don't—"

"Of course, I'll pay you, not much to start—let's think of a couple of days a week for the first month, then we re-evaluate. Anyway, that means we start the design studio in the guesthouse. Mom and dad are back home in Port Gamble. He landed a construction project which gives you and me the second bedroom in the main house. What have you been doing while I was away—commuting from Seattle to the reservation?"

"Yes, I was contemplating renting a room on the reservation, but I felt it would be too close to Hawk and the casino. Might complicate things more than help. I didn't want to upset the tribal elders. So far Hawk's people have accepted me. I called your grandfather a few times—slept in the bunk beds."

"Oh, the bunks. They'll have to go back in storage so we have more room. Enough on the logistics, let's get to the good stuff. Honestly, Maria, once I landed at SeaTac Airport it was if working in Paris was a million years ago. Almost." Gilly closed her eyes, took a deep breath, as she slid her hand over her tummy.

"Anytime you want to talk about the baby, I'll be here for you," Maria said, leaning forward, laying her hand on Gilly's.

"I know you will." Gilly slipped off her shoes digging her heels into a spot of sand. "The adrenalin's really been pumping the last twenty-four hours. Being home, seeing you and my family, and now talking about starting a business … it's thrilling. Scary, but thrilling.

"I've done some research on how other designers began their businesses. Most started with a concept and a few looks telling the story of that concept. The Working Girl shop in Seattle started me down the path of my concept. I didn't realize it at the time what a major impact it made on me. I'll change the words around to *The Career Woman*. What do you think?"

"Keep talking." Maria grinned back.

"Five looks have been swirling in my head—I'll get them on paper and then draw them on my electronic tablet. I learned some tricks from the design staff at one of the fashion houses about using the tablets. It's fabulous the way I can make changes with a stylus, save the file, print the file, whatever."

"Don't forget the copyright notice Hawk gave you."

"Oh, you bet I won't forget that critical piece of information … from my lawyer." The girl's giggled remembering how serious Hawk was about Gilly protecting her designs.

"Any little packages from Edward Churchill?"

"Once. In Paris. Another box with a steel spike through a red heart. It had a Seattle postmark." Gilly looked out at a pleasure boat plowing through the water. "So … I'll have five looks. Start simple and targeted. All suits. The Suit-Dress—a jacket and dress ensemble. A pant, and then a jacket and skirt. Combinations of these will makeup two more looks—mix and match with tops, scarves. Given the timing, this first collection of five looks will be for fall—a year from now—but ready for the shows this spring when buyers make their selections for their fall offerings to the public." Gilly drew the number three in the sand, plus sign, and the number two equaling the number five.

"The Gillianne Wilder label will be synonymous with fine tailoring, quality workmanship with quality fabrics. The woman who buys our clothes will know immediately by the fit that they are experiencing perfection in style and cut. Quality. Quality. Quality. When she looks in her closet, she will naturally gravitate to our clothes because they feel good, sophisticated, sharp, powerful, but always feminine—their go-to look."

"You give me goose bumps. When do I start?"

"You just did. As soon as I have the looks saved in my tablet, you and I will drape muslin on the mannequins, then create patterns, then sew samples. At the same time we have to make calls and interview potential cutting and sewing factories for our first orders. We'll show these initial samples to a Nordstrom's buyer, and I know The Working Girl shop, Stacy Sinclair, will probably put a set on display say in four or five weeks. It's the beginning of winter so jackets will be on the minds of our career women. Accept orders if they come."

"My God, Gilly, this could happen fast. You're going to have to factor in a few weeks for the birth of your baby, and I'll need a couple of weeks to get married."

"You think?" Gilly laughed.

They leaned back, feet outstretched. Still sitting on the log, Gilly looked down. "Maria, look. I'm starting to get a baby bump." Their eyes riveted on Gilly's tummy and then, wide-eyed, looked at each other.

"All I can say is, we'd better get started," Maria said.

Laughing, and not able to sit still, they began walking back to the rickety stairs and the little guesthouse studio.

Chapter 24

Helen Churchill, seventy-four years young, trim, spine straight as an arrow, settled herself on the little chair in the Port Gamble Tea Room. She was excited about showing Anne Wilder the pictures from last April's wedding of her friend's granddaughter in New York City. Gilly had designed and created the dress Helen wore to the event. The wedding was nice, a bit stuffy Helen thought, but she had made quite a stir in her beaded gown.

"Hello, Helen. Spot of tea?" Anne asked holding a china teapot with painted pink roses. "Today's special—strawberry with a touch of lemon."

"Of course, and when you get a minute I have something to show you."

"Now is good. What do you have there?" Anne poured the hot tea into a china cup and set it down in front of her favorite customer.

Helen opened a cream colored, leather-bound book to the page marked with a blue ribbon. "Here. What do you think of this picture?"

Anne slid into the chair beside Helen as the fashionable silver-gray haired lady, her eyes twinkling, turned the book in front of her.

"Oh, Helen, you look so pretty and the gown …" Anne looked up at Helen's beaming face. "The gown is elegant."

The little brass bell hanging from atop the front door jingled as Gilly swept into the cozy tearoom, a smile spreading from ear to ear. Seeing her mother with Helen Churchill, she scooted to the table and slid into the third chair after giving Helen a warm hug of hello.

"You're just in time, honey," Anne said. "Look at this. Helen brought over pictures of the wedding, what? Over a year ago?"

"Yes, I pestered my friend often enough that she finally sent a complete wedding photo album to me. Or, make that loaned it to me."

Helen turned the book again so Gilly could see.

"It's a wonderful picture and, Helen, you look beautiful."

"My gown looks beautiful, my dear."

Anne looked quickly to Gilly. "Was everything okay at the doctor's?"

Concern drew across Helen's face. "Gilly, I hope you're not ill?"

"No, no, Helen. I'm going to have a baby." Gilly's face quickly turned pensive. She was sure Helen was going to ask her about the father. Why did she have to say anything ... she should have waited until she was alone with her mother. But she was so relieved after seeing the doctor that the words just spilled out of her mouth.

Helen glanced at Gilly's hand. "Dear, you're not wearing a ring. You just returned from Paris. Whatever happened to you?"

Gilly quickly told her story and that the father of her baby had been killed. She added that she was beginning to come to grips with his death, but stopped before trying to conjure up a tear. She had no tears for Maxime and certainly wasn't going to pretend now.

"Oh my. How tragic. So, you've come home to live with your family. That's wonderful. Nothing like the support of your mother. Anne, such a horrible story, but you're going to have a grandchild, a baby in the family. That's nice. And, Gilly, when is the little one due to arrive?"

"The doctor thinks the last week in March or first of April. And, Mom, he said I'm on track to have a healthy baby and at my next visit he might be able to determine the sex."

Anne reached over and gave her daughter a hug. "I'm glad everything's okay," she said with a little sigh of relief.

"My, my, how exciting," Helen giggled. "So you must be, what, two months along?"

"Almost three. Nothing fits right ... getting a little tight."

"Living at home I'm sure the little one will thrive, but I'm sorry to hear you're giving up designing."

"Oh, Helen, I'll never give up designing. In fact, I'm working on a five-piece collection. Hope to introduce the samples in a couple of months for buyers to consider in their lineup next fall."

~ ~ ~

Helen was concerned when she heard of Gillianne's plans. Thought they were a bit ambitious, but if anyone could pull it off, Gillianne Wilder could. Settling in her favorite lounger, her husband served their afternoon glass of wine. She told him about her conversation with the Wilder's and added the thought that she wished their grandson Edward had the ambition and drive that Gilly had.

The phone rang. Her husband answered, listened for a minute, and then handed it to her.

"Speak of the devil, it's Edward," he said frowning.

"Hello, Edward, we were just talking about you."

"Something nice I hope, Grandmother."

"You remember Gillianne Wilder … oh dear, of course you do. You had that run in with her and her grandfather. Well she's going to have a baby. I'm not sure I totally understand her story. She returned from Paris without the father. Said he was killed. Sad story really, but she's going ahead with her plans to sometime or other sell her own designs. No thought of putting the baby up for adoption."

Chapter 25

The stars, moon, and sun were in perfect alignment. Gilly felt wonderful. The fields, trees, and farmhouses, beautiful and bright, whizzed by the car windows on the short drive from Port Gamble to Gramp's house. She had pulled off the road twice jotting down notes, adding to her to-do list, drawing lines to reposition the order of the list: see Maria; call Nicole and Sheridan with the good news that she had seen the doctor and she and the baby are fine; ask Nicole to check on three light-weight wools she had seen at a textile factory in Paris.

Gilly dug out her phone and called Maria to see if she could spare thirty minutes if Gilly met her at the spa. Maria said she'd see her in the casino's Longhorn restaurant—call when she arrived. Adding a few more items to her list, Gilly put the car in drive, turned away from Hansville and sped down the road leading to Bainbridge.

Pulling into the parking garage she found a spot close to the elevator, stuffed her notes into her tote, and hustled to the Longhorn Restaurant. "Maria, I'm here. Table to your right."

"Great. I'm on way down."

The girls were hunched over a table in the corner when Hawk walked over to them, kissed his fiancé and planted a quick peck on Gilly's cheek. "Looks like you two are hatching something big I'll leave you alone. Just wanted to say, hi." Hawk left—chitchat was not on their list. They glanced up with a quick smile and then back to their notes.

"I'm running into Seattle," Gilly said, her pen poised over the yellow notepad. "I think I can just catch the two o'clock ferry. I have to pick up a bolt of muslin so we can start the initial samples. Maria, what do you think about a website?"

"We're on the same wave length. I just finished Hawk's. It's not up yet ... waiting to see what his timing is for opening an office in Seattle. I can do the same for you. As soon as we finish sewing a couple of pieces I'll put together your marketing tool—a lookbook with photographs of your collection to show potential buyers when you meet with them. We really need to hire a professional photographer. I'll check who the casino hired for their website, postcards, etcetera—their marketing pieces. Did you call your friend in Paris about the wool?" Maria asked.

"Not yet. I'll call her from the ferry on my way back from the fabric warehouse. As I mentioned, the fabrics must be a very good quality—some stretch for our career gals, but not outrageously expensive."

Maria added a note to her list, looked up shaking her pen between her fingers releasing pent-up energy. "I made a list of some of the words you used when we talked on the beach. I want to incorporate them into the descriptions of the looks. And, I definitely want to feature the jackets. Who knows they may become your signature item—fabulous linings that tease the eye and surprise colleagues when our gal casually sheds the jacket to a chair revealing the gorgeous lining."

"Maria, what does Hawk think about all this ... and my baby?"

"Sad. Surprised. Delighted. Sees a new client when you form your corporation?" Maria laughed. "I think in sound bites now."

"Love it. I'd better get going or I'll miss the ferry." Gilly started to leave, stopped and finished the last drop of milk in her glass. "Do you think you could call the Design Academy to get some leads on cutting and sewing factories in Seattle?" Gilly asked smiling.

"What are you smiling about?" Maria asked.

"Just thinking about our instructor, old Ms. Crochet. I wonder what she'd say if she knew that *we* teamed up, *and* what we are planning."

"When *we* make our first sale, or debut in the newspaper, I'll send her a signed clipping."

"Be sure to add COO after your name," Gilly said.

"COO?"

"Chief Operating Officer."

"Wow. You mean it?" Maria asked.

"You bet. A high-paid COO."

"How about just *a paid COO*."

The girls giggled clasping hands around each other and then Gilly dashed off to catch the ferry leaving Maria adding to her to-do list: cutting and sewing factories.

Chapter 26

Calls bounced between Gilly's and Maria's cell phones. Items crossed off one to-do list landed on another. New items added to both. Tasks accomplished were removed altogether with a trail of notes detailing what was done, how, and when.

Gilly skillfully moved the stylus over the screen drawing the finishing touches to the five-piece collection. Leaning back in the chair she rubbed her lower back while tilting the electronic sketchpad up in front of her. This afternoon she planned to start draping the muslin sample on Patty, the mannequin. The bolt of muslin she bought in Seattle a week ago was propped up in the corner of the guesthouse living room—her makeshift studio.

Hearing a car door close and a dog barking racing from the driveway to the patio, she knew instantly who had just reappeared in her life.

A man's shadow jogged by the window.

Skip.

The dog continued to bark at the patio door demanding attention.

Coco, asleep in a ray of sun, slid out the guesthouse cat door to join her doggie friend.

Gilly knew it had to happen sometime but she wasn't ready to face him. She wasn't sure how she felt about him. Before leaving for Paris they had grown close. Even to the point that she had let the idea of their becoming intimate enter her mind. But she left for Paris and Maxime had swept the thought of any other man away. She had come to the realization—too late—that he just wanted another conquest. A stupid, naive, girl from the western sticks of Washington didn't have a chance against a charming, handsome Frenchman. A worldly man who knew how to manipulate a woman, never mind a girl of twenty-three.

She heard Gramps greet his friend. Skip Hunter. Seattle Times' reporter. Oh, dear God, what am I going to say, she thought. Putting both hands around her belly, she believed she could pass off most comments by merely suggesting she had put on weight. But Skip would think differently. His reporter's eye would guess her secret whether he said so or not. If he had any feelings for her before, he would certainly throw them away once he saw her condition.

~ ~ ~

"Agatha, my friend." Gramps opened the patio door and the exuberant Bassett Hound kissed the face bent to her, then instantly rolled over on her back, four paws in the air waiting for her belly rub. "Yes, yes. There you are. Missed me did you? Come on in, Skip. I'll shake your hand in a minute after I attend to my dog here."

Gripping the edge of the nearby table for help, Gramps stood up, shook Skip's hand and motioned for him to come in. "Took you long enough to get over here. I was about to call you."

"Hi, Clay. What do you mean took me long enough?"

"Oh, my, now we're going to be formal are we—vague, pretend we don't know a certain granddaughter of mine is back in town. I thought you were calling me Gramps but we're back to Clay. At least you didn't revert to Mr. Wilder." Gramps chuckled. "Tea?"

"Love a cup." In the kitchen, Gramps put two cups and saucers on the table, Skip sat gazing out at Puget Sound. Agatha flopped in her favorite place—half in the living room, the front half in the kitchen watching the action as Coco touched noses, then curled up next to Agatha's ample girth.

"Gilly's up in her studio."

"Studio?" Skip took a sip of the lemon-ginger concoction.

"Guesthouse living room. She and Maria have taken over the place. So?"

"So? What?"

"What took you so long? I presume someone, probably Maria, let you know that Gilly was back. Did she say anything else?" Gramps asked searching Skip's face for any knowledge of Gilly's pending event.

"Maria did mention Gilly was back. I happened to bump into her and Hawk at Ivar's having a drink while they waited for the ferry."

"Well, when you finish that tea you best go up and break the ice. Seems a little tension has crept in since she left here back in March."

"Not as far as I'm concerned … guess that's not quite true. When I went to Paris to witness the arrest of Mrs. Wellington I stopped by Gilly's apartment. Did she tell you?"

"No, she didn't. Did you see her?"

"No, she was out of town but her roommates and I had a cup of coffee together. I got the distinct impression that Gilly was seeing someone. In fact, it sounded to me like she had gone away for a few days with him. Has she said anything to you about a man?"

"Yes, she has but I'll let her tell you. Skip, Gilly's changed…and I don't just mean physically. Give her a chance, son."

"You're talking in riddles. I'll go up and talk to her … break that ice," Skip said with a grin. "Okay if Agatha stays with you? I'll get her when I leave."

"Of course. I think I have one of those rawhide bones hidden away just waiting for her to visit me."

~ ~ ~

Gilly looked up hearing the scratch of the intercom.

"Gilly, Skips on his way up."

"Okay, thanks, Gramps."

Her chest tightened, held her breath as Skip's shadow passed the window. He opened the door and stepped in. Gilly stood with her back to him, hands tight across her middle, eyes closed as she faced the far wall.

"Hi, Gilly. Gramps said I should come up. Hope you don't mind—"

Gilly slowly turned around letting her hands hang to her side. "Hello, Skip." Breathing came in short bursts, her mouth slightly open, words were impossible.

Skip looked at her, taking in the slight swell of her belly. He looked to her face, his blue eyes questioning what he saw in front of him. "I didn't know you were married. Your roommates didn't—"

She wanted to bury her face in his chest. Wanted him to wrap his arms around her as he had done before. Comforting her, Protecting her. Telling her everything would be all right. But she had no right to ask. Wait. What was she thinking? She didn't want him back in her life again. She didn't want any man. She didn't want any man to enter her life ever.

Afraid to speak, she raised her left hand showing him that her ring finger was bare.

"I don't understand," he said sitting in the plastic garden chair at the end of the long table. She had made no move toward him. In fact he felt a distinct wall of ice go up between them. "Are you just going to stand there, or are you going to tell me what happened in Paris?" Skip spit out the words, words that felt like darts hitting her body.

So what. She didn't care. "Not a whole lot to tell." Gilly picked up her half finished glass of milk willing herself to breathe long and deep. She drank the milk, put the glass down, faced him.

"The short version, the only version, is that I met a Frenchman. It was love at first sight. We planned to marry after he returned from a government assignment but he was killed. I came home to start my business."

"That's it? That story rolled off your tongue rather easily—like a marketing pitch in an elevator. There's more. What is it?"

Gilly saw his temper rising. His blue eyes turning flinty. She's was glad because it made it easier for her to snap back in return. He had a nerve questioning what she said. So what if he didn't believe her? "There isn't any more. He's dead and I'm home and, as you can see, I'm working hard getting my business started. Maria is—"

"If that's all you're going to tell me, then I think I'd better be going." Skip strode out, down the three steps, more long strides to the patio door, jerked it open and swung around. Gilly stood outside the guesthouse door, arms crossed, glaring at him.

"When's the baby due?" he spat out.

"April Fool's day." She saw him blanch like the wind had been knocked out of him. He looked up at her, his eyes full of hurt as he entered the patio slamming the door behind him.

Gilly stepped back into the guesthouse slamming the door in retaliation. She stood staring at the closed door, sparks flying from her eyes, her lungs screaming for air. She saw his shadow pass the window as Coco darted in the cat door, jumped up and squirmed to the sunshine behind the curtain watching Agatha scamper into the car.

Gilly imagined him getting into his jeep, heard the engine turnover, the car quietly pulled out of the driveway and up the road, the sound of the engine fading to nothing.

Gilly flopped down in the chair, elbows on the table holding her head. Coco fished her way out from behind the curtain, brushed her mistress's arm, purring.

Feeling a tear stinging her eye, Gilly's head snapped up. "NO. NO. Stop it, Gillianne Wilder. Get back to work. NOW, Gillianne! NOW!" she shouted. Her words a clear rebuke to the tear and any that might follow.

Picking up the stylus, she made a slight correction to the black jacket on the screen of her electronic tablet.

Chapter 27

Paris

Edward Churchill hobbled onto the Air France jet bound for Paris and settled his slight frame into the first-class window seat. His funds were running low but he splurged on the upgraded fare, after all he was a Churchill, and Churchill's were accustomed to first-class travel. Edward figured his father had found out his mother was routinely depositing money into their son's bank account as her routine had become sporadic. No matter, his account would soon be fat again, and, if things worked out, money might be deposited regularly from another source, maybe two other sources, well into the future.

The stewardess handed Edward his complementary drink as well as the dinner menu. He smiled thinking about the poor suckers in the rear cabin—they had to pay for everything and endure the cramped seating. Edward fished out a little pill case from his breast pocket and downed two capsules with his boilermaker—a whiskey with beer chaser. After dinner he'd go over his list of the top five fashion houses once more and then sleep for the long flight into Charles de Gaulle Airport.

The travel agent had made reservations for him at a hotel in the fashion district. After a catnap he'd begin his search for the father of Gilly's baby. He figured given the short period of time she was in Paris that it must have been a torrid affair and someone at where she worked would be aware of the hot redhead from the States involved in a hot affair.

Following his plan, Edward stepped from plane to cab to hotel in record time. Refreshed from a two-hour nap and a shower, he headed to the first company on his list. He had his story—he was returning to the States from the battlefield of Afghanistan where he was wounded in the foot. He was looking for his sister. He wanted to see her before heading home to his mother and father and much needed therapy and rest from his ordeal.

His first stop was good and bad. Good because the personnel manager had teared up hearing his story and wished she could help him. Looking up Gillianne Wilder on her computer, she was sorry, but no one by that name appeared. She did, however, give him another company to add to his list. Thanking her, he limped from her office, obviously in more pain from his wound than when he entered. Passing a café he thought about stopping for an afternoon drink, but postponed the urge. He didn't want to have liquor on his breath when he was asking for his dear sister; although no one would have blamed him for having a drink or two given he was fresh from the war zone.

Company two had no record of a Gillianne Wilder and was *so so* sorry to disappoint him. The woman helped him as he limped to the front entrance wishing him well.

He hit the mother lode at company three. The personnel manager was out but her assistant, a gabby forty-something French woman in spike heels and tight dress providing a view to her ample cleavage, found G. Wilder on the first pass.

"Yes, your sister works here … oh, wait a minute, there's a note that she is no longer available. I'm not sure what that means. I'll write down the name and number of her agent. Maybe she can help you."

"Thank you, Madame, that would be helpful. Maybe she took a job somewhere else."

"She's certainly a pretty thing. Her picture … I've seen her. Oh my, yes, she's the one."

"Excuse me, *the one*?" Edward asked his heart skipping a beat. This old lady knows something, he thought. Easy, Edward, don't spook her.

The woman looked up from under her fresh set of long eyelashes applied that morning. She gave a furtive look at the office door and quickly closed it. "Your sister had us all panting."

"My goodness," Edward giggled. "Why was that?"

"Maxime Beaumont. He saw her one afternoon modeling a gown, a very revealing gown I was told. And he pounced. So to speak."

"Madame, are you saying Monsieur Beaumont pounced like in asked her out?"

"Oh, my yes. He pursued her. Whenever she modeled for us he was there. One of the fitters caught them in a very compromising kiss. Whew, he causes my heart to race just thinking about him. I'm not surprised your sister didn't tell you about him after all he is a married man. She suddenly disappeared. Maybe she went back to the States. Her agent, the number I gave you, probably knows how to reach Ms. Wilder if she's still in Paris. Of course, your parents must know where she is."

Edward leaned in. "Maybe she doesn't want to be found … you know ran off with this Beaumont fella."

"I don't think so. I saw an article in the paper the other day. He's running for the Senate next spring."

~ ~ ~

Edward sat in the corner of a cozy café near his hotel giggling to himself, smiling from ear to ear as he nursed his second whiskey, straight up. He would have bet every penny he had that the father of Gilly's baby was Beaumont, and when she told the creep about the baby he dropped her like a hot potato. Mulling over his next step he flagged the waitress and ordered a steak, rare, with mushrooms. Forget the salad. He needed something hearty to flesh out his plans for Beaumont.

Finished with his dinner Edward strolled back to his hotel—the pain barely noticeable he was so preoccupied, and numbed with liquor. He had mapped out his strategy to get the biggest payout possible from the man running for the Senate, a man who could not stand to have a scandal erupt. Of course, European men were known for their mistresses, but an American mistress with child, that was different. Ohhh yeahhh. This was going to be easy.

~ ~ ~

Edward limped into Beaumont's office at ten o'clock the next morning—late enough the man would be in, but early enough he wouldn't be out to lunch or a meeting. He had dressed carefully—suit and tie, his best black Italian shoes. Beaumont was not going to take him for some bum off the street. No, Beaumont would recognize Edward as a significant adversary.

The receptionist scanned her boss's calendar, but didn't see an appointment with an Edward Churchill.

"I'm sorry, Monsieur Churchill. There seems to be no appointment today with your name. Perhaps you would like to schedule an appointment for another day?"

"Please give Monsieur Beaumont my name. Tell him I have the information he requested concerning a June baby. I think he'll see me."

"Well…"

"Just tell him, s'il vous plaît."

The young woman hesitated then decided to speak with her boss. Surely he'd tell her to get rid of the man. She stepped into Beaumont's office with Edward's request to see him. To her surprise, her boss looked up sharply from the report he was preparing for his father.

"Show the man in. I'll get rid of him."

Edward strolled into Beaumont's office hiding his limp, sucking up the pain at the same time taking in the sumptuous furnishings, the gleaming mahogany floor-to-ceiling bookcases filled with law books, the oriental rugs over plush carpets, and the heavy tapestry drapes. He knew he stood in a room filled with great wealth. He extended his hand to Beaumont who remained seated behind his desk, and then flopped in a chair a pain darting up his leg.

"What is it you wanted to see me about? My receptionist indicated it was urgent," Beaumont asked, leaning forward in his black-leather chair, elbows on his desk. He sat in his shirtsleeves, a black silk suit jacket placed carefully on a hanger Edward saw on the open door of a closet.

Edward sized the man up. Figured Beaumont to be in his mid- to late-thirties, and oh yes, he was a handsome Frenchman. Women probably fell all over themselves to do his bidding especially a young stupid girl from the sticks of Western Washington. A girl like Gilly. "I have a deal for you, one I'm sure you'll be very interested in accepting."

"What kind of a deal?" Maxime scrutinized the skinny fellow facing him—June baby? No way. The guy looked nothing like Gillianne so he couldn't be a relative. Nonetheless, Maxime's heart rate rose.

"Something you want in return for something I want," Edward said quietly his tone firm with a hint of conspiracy.

"And what do you want, Monsieur Churchill?"

"One million Euros."

Beaumont chuckled. "And what could I possibly want from you for such a sum?" My God, he thought. Such a large amount. He must think I'm an easy mark or … or … he knows something. A tick in Maxime's left eyelid accompanied his elevating pulse.

"My silence." Edward paused seeing the nervous twitch in Beaumont's eye. "For my silence regarding your bastard baby Gillianne

Wilder is carrying. My silence that the story will not appear in the media—the newspapers, television, radio, tabloids, and no tipoff to the paparazzi devils."

Chapter 28

Seattle

The sidewalks of downtown Seattle were teaming with office workers, shoppers, and tourists. Gripping her rolling suitcase containing the precious first presentation of her five-piece collection Gilly weaved through the throng to her first appointment. She hoped her lookbook of sketches would entice the two people she was meeting with to ask to see samples. If asked she and her mom and Maria would somehow produce them.

Her meeting with Stacy Sinclair, owner of the Working Girl shop, was a bit nostalgic but she also felt she had an edge. After all, Stacy had displayed three of her fall looks following Gilly's success modeling the pieces in her store.

Taking a deep breath, Gilly pushed through the plate-glass doors a big smile on her face. It felt good to be back in the pretty little shop. It was in a good location—a block from Nordstrom's Department Store.

"My dear dear Gillianne." Stacy rushed up to Gilly, blowing a kiss on each cheek as she embraced her. "You look fabulous." Pushing Gilly away at arm's length, Stacy's eyes popped as she took in Gilly's baby bump. "Gilly, are you pregnant? Did some Frenchman sweep you off your feet? Come, come out back and tell me." Stacy guided Gilly to the back room, pointed to a chair and looked at Gilly expectantly.

Gilly was ready. She had anticipated the question, rehearsing her answer several times on the ferry crossing the sound this morning.

"Yes," Gilly said in a light tone of voice. "Yes, to all of the above. However, before we could get married, he was killed in a tragic accident." She pulled a small, white linen handkerchief from her tote, the one she had put there to dab a non-existent tear from her eye, then tucked the hanky back in her pocket.

"Oh, how awful. You poor thing. How did it happen?"

"Stacy, someday I'll be strong enough to talk about it, but right now, I'm trying to forget my loss and concentrate on the little miracle I'm carrying." She smiled brightly, "And," she whispered, "I'm concentrating on my new business."

Just as Gilly had hoped, the questions stopped. The subject switched back to the purpose of her meeting—the presentation of her collection.

Opening her case she withdrew the lookbook she and Maria had sweated over featuring three looks, and a companion book with two looks, with sample swatches for each piece. She wasn't sure at the time why they had split the collection into a group of three and another of two—more impressive maybe.

She handed Stacy the three-piece lookbook.

"Gilly, I really like this jacket, and the companion pieces—so sophisticated yet comfortable." Stacy caressed the jacket's fabric swatch between her fingers. "These pieces are for fall and winter. When do you think they will be ready for display? For sale?" Stacy asked, turning the page.

"I know I'm late, but I thought some of your clients who bought my fall designs last October at the show might be ready to add to their wardrobe, you know spice it up with a few new pieces. With the cold weather in Seattle, women still have several months, four or five, of the coldest weather ahead before spring arrives. I could have samples for you to display in a week, and then items of a few sizes to sell the following week. Two seamstresses are helping me with the samples. And, Stacy, I'm demanding quality workmanship and superior tailoring. If you don't agree, that the pieces are of the highest quality you have ever seen, I won't bother you again."

"I believe you, dear. The three orders you filled after my little fashion show … well, the women still rave about the pieces and actually have asked me about you over the summer."

Excitement shot through Gilly. Stacy's reaction to her drawings was even better than she had hoped for.

"Tell you what I'll do," Stacy said. "You deliver samples of each of these designs as fast as you can and I'll clear a spot in the window featuring your collection. We'll have to decide on the price points, of course, and you must give me a timeframe to fill any orders." Stacy closed the book and handed it along with the swatches back to Gilly. "Mind you, most items sell off-the-rack, so this is a little different for me. But, it's a start."

"Stacy, thank you. It's more than a start. I'll do everything in my power to see that I fulfill the quality you are expecting."

"When is your baby due, dear?"

"End of March."

"You've put yourself on a very ambitious path, Gilly. Take care of yourself. Unfortunately, in the retail business there isn't any room for slack in promised delivery dates."

~ ~ ~

Going up the elevator to the top floor at Nordstrom's, Gilly didn't dare try the escalator with her rolling suitcase fearing with her excitement she'd trip thinking about what Stacy had said regarding making a commitment to a delivery schedule. Yet she didn't hesitate to ask for display samples right away. She also decided Nordstrom's wouldn't want to carry clothing available at a boutique down the street. Gilly decided to show Nordstrom's buyer the lookbook containing two looks, holding the three Stacy saw separate … an exclusive for each retailer.

Her appointment with the Nordstrom buyer didn't go as well. The woman was very busy, constantly taking phone calls and there were many interruptions by staff popping in and out with questions. However, the buyer seemed intrigued with the lookbook and the fact that Gilly had won the competition the store sponsored almost a year ago. She particularly liked the second look—same jacket featured with a pair of flattering pants and then coupled with a knockout cocktail dress for that party after work. The cropped jacket was reversible, giving a shimmery, glamorous look for evening. Holding the book at an angle, she covered the phone's mouth-piece, looked up over her glasses and addressed Gilly.

"Ms. Wilder, you bring me these two looks as soon as you can. I'll put them in our women's career department. Who knows, we may have some takers for the holidays." She smiled and returned to her phone call, waving goodbye to Gilly, and turning her attention to her Blackberry calendar.

Gilly sailed down the elevator and out one of the main entrances with the desire to hug everyone walking by the store. She was one of them—a business woman with two verbal requests for samples of her collection. Flagging down a cab, she felt as if nothing could stop her now. She had to call Maria but decided to wait until she was on the ferry to relay her news besides she had to bring her adrenalin under control. Thankfully she had opted to take the ferry as a foot passenger so she didn't have to deal with her car until she was on the other side of the sound. She paid the cab and hustled onboard the ferry loaded with commuters.

Sliding into one of the window booths, she pulled her case tight to her leg, gripped her tote against her side, and laid her head back closing her eyes. What a trip, she thought. Snapping to attention, she placed her call to Maria.

"Hey, girl friend, how did it go in the big city?" Maria asked.

"Absolutely terrific. Just wait till I fill you in. I need to meet with you *and* Hawk together because I'll run out of steam if I have to tell everything more than once. Can I stop by the casino and meet you guys for dinner? I'm on the ferry and should dock within the hour."

"Hang on."

Gilly heard some mumbling and pictured Maria on the other end of the line. She was probably with Hawk.

"Hawk said that works. He's buying. Actually, I said that, he didn't, but he's nodding yes. Can you give me a clue what we're meeting about?"

"Oh, just a couple of little things—incorporating my business, legalities around taking and delivering orders for my collection, and how much time he'll let me steal my COO away to sew 24/7 over the next week."

Chapter 29

What a day!

An exciting day.

Dusk settled over Puget Sound cloaking Gramp's house in shadows. Gilly trotted gaily down the steps to the patio, blood coursing through her body.

"Hi, Gramps, I'm home," she called out shedding her jacket in what was now officially her bedroom.

"Come eat. Your mom brought over a pot of our favorite beef stew."

Catching Gramps ladling stew into the bowls, she planted a kiss on his cheek. "Umm, smells divine. Make mine a small bowl. I had a bite to eat with Hawk and Maria but I'm still hungry."

"Had a good day did you?" He chuckled as he placed the steamy bowls of stew on the green laminated table alongside a basket of chewy French bread.

"Just wait till I tell you."

"A package came for you today … from Paris. It's on the dryer," he said spreading butter on a chunk of bread.

Gilly picked up the book-sized parcel wrapped in brown paper. "No return address. Probably something from Nicole … or Sheridan." She tore the paper away revealing a white box and lifted the lid.

"No!" The word strangled as her throat constricted.

Gramps eyes darted to the open box—a steel spike through a red satin heart. "Sweetie, there's a folded piece of paper underneath." He picked up the heart and handed Gilly the paper, replacing the ill-omened heart, and closed the box.

Her fingers shaking, Gilly tried to unfold the paper.

"Here, let me see that." Gramps took the paper from her hand, adjusted the glasses on his nose, and read the letter to her.

"Dear Bitch, Congratulations on the pending birth of your child. Clever as I am, I deduced you must have met up with a Frenchman in the city of love—your love. Tsk Tsk.

I was so excited for you that I flew to Paris to congratulate the daddy. Seems your telling everyone a story, a fabricated story that the father of your baby is dead. Now, you and I know that's not true.

I'm a little short of funds but I figure that twenty-thousand dollars would help me to re-establish myself. I think I'll stay in Paris for awhile. One of the fashion houses, the one where you modeled and, oh yes, the one where you met the man who fathered your child, indicated they might be interested in my designs.

So, Bitch, you send me the money and I will remain silent.

Oh, I have news for you—your baby's daddy announced he is running for the Senate and this piece of tawdry information would certainly help his opponent's campaign don't you think?

You'll receive instructions on where to wire my payment shortly. Have a nice day.

Spiky."

Gramps slowly refolded the letter, returned it to the box, and replaced the lid. Glancing at Gilly staring glassy-eyed into her bowl of stew, all color had drained from her face, her body twitching sporadically as she tried to stop shaking.

"Do you want to tell me what happened in Paris?" he said softly, covering her hand and firmly pulling her back from the scenes playing out in her mind.

Gilly slowly raised her head, her pained eyes seeking her grandfather's, pleading for understanding.

"I thought I loved him … I thought he loved me. I was wrong," she whispered gulping for air. "How could I have been so blind, so stupid, Gramps?"

"You're a beautiful young woman, Gillianne. You have the talent and drive to become whatever you want. Matters of the heart are complex. Your moral compass—what's right or wrong—sometimes becomes overwhelmed by emotions that engulf your body. You find yourself in a tailspin that you can't pull out of. You were riding high—beautiful city, the fashion world opening up to you laying all the possibilities you had dreamed of at your feet. Then a man comes along, your defenses are down. At that moment you feel anything and everything is possible, is real."

Gilly's eyes filled, a teardrop fell to her lap as she lowered her head.

"Gramps, I learned he was married … after. He said they lead separate lives. That he thought about getting a divorce. … but it was too late."

"Did you tell him? Does he know you're pregnant?"

Gilly dabbed at her eyes. "I was about to tell him but he said he had something to tell me. I stupidly thought he was going to say he was getting a divorce. I urged him to tell me his news first."

Gramps pushed his stew bowl aside. "His news?"

"That he was running for the Senate, that he and his wife had reconciled, that she was going to stand by him."

"And you…"

"I said goodbye … I walked home. That's when my roommates helped me come up with my story."

"So, he doesn't know your carrying his child?"

Gilly shook her head. "What am I going to do?" she whispered.

Gramp's pulled his plaid, man-sized handkerchief from his pocket and pushed it into her palm.

"Edward Churchill doesn't know who he's messing with, child. Blackmail is a crime. You need the advice of a lawyer. One thing is for sure. You are not going to give in to this threat." He gripped her small delicate hand between his large weathered hands, arthritis creeping into some of his fingers.

Gilly raised her head, feeling the strength of her grandfather flowing from his hands to hers. "I love you Gramps."

"I love you to, sweetie." He patted her arm, picked up his spoon and scooped up a mouthful of stew. The ache he felt for what lay ahead of his treasured granddaughter caused his shoulders to slump slightly with fatigue. Gilly walked to the telephone mounted on the wall and dialed the number for the casino. "Hello, Mr. Hawk Jackson, please." She leaned against the wall, waiting for the connection. "Hi, Hawk."

"Gilly, what's the matter?"

"I need your help."

"I know. Since you left us I've put together a couple of ideas for you … on forming your company—"

"Hawk," Gilly cut in. "Remember that jewelry box I received at the dinner party Gramps threw for me at the Space Needle after winning the competition?"

"Yes. That stupid spike in a red heart."

"I just received another one. Can you and Maria meet me tomorrow morning? I can come to the casino, but it has to be private. I'm in trouble, Hawk."

"Of course. Would you rather we come to Hansville, say ten o'clock?"

"Yes. Thank you." Gilly hung up the receiver.

"Gramps, I'm not hungry. I think I'll go to bed."

Chapter 30

Raindrops splattered against the window as Gilly clutched the covers, pulling them over her shoulders, up under her chin. She knew she was in terrible trouble and it was only the beginning. Gramps was right, she was going to end up talking to the police, which meant the truth would come out, which meant Maxime was probably going to hear about the baby. What if she had to fight him for her baby … all of his money?

Sleep came in fits and starts. She woke feeling nauseous, hurried down the hall in her bare feet to the bathroom. Maybe a bout of morning sickness, or nerves, she thought. Probably both. Lifting her head from the toilet bowl, she remained sitting on the tile floor, leaning against the cabinets, waiting to see if she was done heaving. Resting several minutes, feeling the lurching of her stomach had calmed down, she struggled to her feet, turned on the shower. Stepping in, hands out to brace herself, she stood letting the hot water warm her skin, the chills and shaking melting away. Her eyes and mind began to focus forming a list of questions to be addressed with Hawk. Hawk! Thank God for him and Maria.

She dressed, took the cup of tea Gramps extended to her, and left the house for her studio. A little before ten o'clock she heard Hawk's SUV pull into the driveway. Willing her nerves to remain calm she greeted them at the door holding it open as they scurried inside out of the rain.

Hawk and Maria exchanged glances after seeing how Gilly looked—a completely different woman than the one filled with exuberance in anticipation of launching her business the day before. Maria embraced Gilly briefly sensing how upset her friend was but not knowing the reason behind the urgent call.

"There's coffee on the counter if you like," Gilly said opening two folding chairs and sitting down in one. Coco vacated the garden chair and curled up in Gilly's lap.

Ignoring the offer, Hawk sat down beside Gilly. She said nothing just pushed the small box from the middle of the long folding table to Hawk indicating with a nod that he should open it. Maria stood behind him, watching over his shoulder.

Hawk quickly opened the box, let out a sigh at the sight of the heart with the spike stabbed in the center. He then unfolded the letter and he and Maria read the threat.

Maria moved behind Gilly, leaned over and wrapped her arms around her, laying her head against her mop of red hair. "I'm so sorry. You should have told us. You know we love you."

"I know," Gilly whispered.

"From your reaction, I take it what this letter alleges is true?" Hawk asked.

Gilly nodded.

"What's this *daddy's* name?"

"Maxime Beaumont."

"And, if you've been sticking to your story, how does this Spiky guy know about the father, and how did he find out his name?"

"Once I began thinking about how he could have possible found out, it was pretty easy to come up with the answer. The day I went to see the doctor for the first time, I was excited to learn that both the baby and I were fine. I went to the tearoom to see my mother. She was talking to Helen Churchill, Spiky's grandmother. Mom asked me about the doctor, Helen asked me if I was sick, and hence the story. She must have told her grandson. If what he says in the note is true about finding the fashion house where I did some modeling, all he had to do was mention my name and they would have relayed the gossip about my seeing Maxime. Thinking back, I'm sure they all knew he was married but neglected to tell me that *little* fact."

A puff of air escaped Hawk's mouth. "Okay then, does this Maxime know you're pregnant?"

"No. He doesn't. When I met Maxime to tell him, he started talking about how he and his wife had reconciled and that he was going to run for the Senate, and … I just stood up, said goodbye, and left him. Left him as in forever."

"Gilly, this is blackmail and blackmail is a felony." Hawk helped himself to coffee, turned his chair round and sat straddling the seat to face his client. You have to go to the police."

Gilly straightened in her chair, her spine slowly stiffened like a ramrod. "Deputy Kracker? In Bremerton?"

"No. What's the name of the police detective who Skip shadowed for his story on the gold robbery?"

"Detective DuBois."

"Yeah, him. Seattle detective. He may even get the Feds involved. Do you have the wrapping this box came in?"

Gilly leaned over and pushed the brown paper to Hawk. Coco fell off her lap, sat licking her paw, and then jumped up on the garden chair.

"Paris postmark. No return address. He's from New York isn't he?"

"Yes, the city."

"And he tried to strangle you as I recall when your grandfather shot at him. This man he mentions in the letter—"

"Maxime Beaumont. He's a corporate lawyer in a family practice. His grandfather founded the firm in Paris."

"You're sure he's the father of your baby?"

"Hawk," Marie glared.

"Yes. He's the father."

Hawk felt better hearing Gilly's voice gaining strength. "I don't want to cause you more alarm, but if Spiky tells Beaumont he's a father to-be, what do you think he'd do? I'll give you the answer. I don't think he'll leave his wife, fly to Seattle, and ask you to marry you."

"What are you saying?" Maria asked.

"He could come after you, not to ask you to marry him but to cause you harm. Have you told your parents about him?"

"No. My two roommates helped me with my story that the father was dead. They are the only ones who know I'm pregnant. Then Gramps last night when I opened the box. He read the letter to me, and now you two."

"Your parents are wonderful," Maria said her voice strong belying the doubt creeping in. "They'll understand … after they digest the truth."

"Understand? Mom … probably. Dad, I don't know."

"Well, ladies, I have to get back to the reservation so to speak," Hawk chuckled hoping to lighten the mood.

"I'll see if I can meet with DuBois tomorrow," Gilly said.

"Good, Put that box and the wrapping paper in a zip-lock bag." Hawk winked at Gilly. "Evidence. Who knows. Maybe the creep is bluffing."

"I'm staying to help Gilly. We need to get going with the samples for the collection," Maria said. "Everything is under control at the spa." Turning to Gilly, she added, "I followed Hawk's suggestion and hired an assistant a few days ago, which reminds me, Gillianne, we have some news for you."

"Good I hope," Gilly said looking up at Maria.

"Very good. We've set the date for our wedding." Maria bent down and kissed Hawk's cheek.

"And?" Gilly said.

"Two days before Christmas. I know, I know, it's not far off, but we want a small wedding on the reservation and there's really only my mom and stepfather on my side."

Gilly stood and threw her arms around Maria in bear hug. "That's wonderful. I'm so happy for you both." What a storyline, Gilly thought. She and Maria met on their first day at design school, Maria dropped out of school meeting Hawk one day with Gilly, she started working at the spa, and now ... a wedding.

"We have to talk," Maria said. "Lay out your plans for when, or if, you're still thinking of moving the studio to Seattle. Hawk found office space he likes. His business is expanding outside the tribe, and an office in the city will work—closer to his contacts at the gaming commission. And, wonderful man he is, he found an apartment for us. I haven't seen it yet—except the pictures on the computer. It looks perfect."

"Oh, I wish I could move as fast," Gilly replied. "I mentioned weeks ago, Maria, that I had contacted a realtor. She keeps calling me about one space after another. She came up with one a few days ago that looked perfect. I just don't have the money yet. But I'm not giving up."

Hawk stood, set his coffee mug in the sink and gave his fiancé a warm embrace. "I'm sure the two of you will come up with something. I have total faith in both of you."

Hawk turned to Gilly, placed his hands on her shoulders. "You should talk to Skip."

"No, no. I can't."

"I'm tied up for a couple of days so I can't go with you to see DuBois but Skip could I'm sure."

"Oh, Hawk, I can't. He …"

"*He* needs to know the truth, Gilly. You owe him that much don't you think?"

Chapter 31

The sewing machines hummed incessantly the rest of the morning, stopping only when Gilly or Maria took her foot of the pedal for a quick drink of coffee or milk. Hawk's words repeated in Gilly's head until she wanted to cover her ears. *What would Maxime do if he found out she was pregnant?*

He might challenge the statement. Being a lawyer, he would know that would be a losing argument. Harm her? Surely he wouldn't be that cruel. Milan had to mean something to him didn't it?

Then there was Skip. Last time they talked he stormed away knowing she was lying to him. But the truth? How could she ask him for his help? But she also didn't want to face DuBois alone. Hawk wanted to accompany her—a lawyer protecting the interests of his client. But she wasn't really a client. Not yet. No money to pay him … yet. She was merely going to see DuBois to put the threat she had received in front of him, ask his advice on what she should do and what role would the police play?

Maria purposely didn't quiz Gilly about what she was going to do. She knew her friend had to have time to think. Maria's only words were to ask Gilly to check the muslin sample of look number three—were the darts deep enough or too deep, did the collar fold as she wanted, did the drape of the dress flow as she envisioned?

Gilly finally stood, stretched, and rubbed her lower back. She looked at Maria bent over her sewing machine watching the pounding needle as she fed the fabric under the foot.

"Hey," Gilly said with a smile.

"Hey what?" Maria replied without looking up.

"Let's break for lunch, get out of here for an hour. What would you say to a cup of tea and a turkey wrap at the Tea Room?"

Maria's foot immediately lifted from the foot pedal. "I'd say, I thought you'd never ask. Let's go."

Gilly pulled on her sweater, grabbed her purse, and the pair stepped out the door inhaling the fresh air washed with the morning's rain.

Sitting down in the homey environs of the Port Gamble Tea Room, light pink walls punctuated with white lace curtains, they gave their order to Anne after a brief hug from each girl. When she returned with the pot of tea, Gilly tugged at her mom's arm pulling her close. "Mom, can you and dad come over to Gramp's for dinner tonight? I have to talk to you both."

"Of course, sweetheart. I'll have time to make a chicken potpie this afternoon—I'll bring it along." Anne patted her daughter's shoulder and moved on to the next table as Maria poured the tea.

The little brass bell tinkled as Helen Churchill bustled in with a couple of plastic bags marked *Port Gamble General Store*. Gilly's hand darted to Maria's arm. Maria looked up following Gilly's look of alarm. Seeing Gilly, Helen made a bee-line to her table. "Gillianne, can I share a bite of lunch with you?" Not waiting for an answer she plopped down, setting her purse and packages on the chair next to her. "Tell me, how is everything? You look grand. Being pregnant suits you. Maria, nice to see you." Helen thanked Anne for the tea and ordered a tuna-salad sandwich. "You girls are quiet. Penny for your thoughts?"

Gilly took a sip of tea. "Helen, have you talked to Edward recently?"

"No … well, he called just before you returned from Paris … or was it just after … sometime around then. Why?"

"Oh, just wondering if he went back to New York. He and I had a nasty scene."

"Oh, I know. I'm so sorry. That boy can be so headstrong. Spoiled rotten by that mother of his. I don't understand how our son could let his wife get away with coddling the boy the way she does. He lost his job you know, and as far as I can see he has no intention of looking for another one."

Gilly and Maria exchanged a quick glance cradling their warm teacups.

Helen looked at the pair with sad eyes. That grandson of hers was a ner-do-well. Hearing about his attack on Gilly, and that her grandfather stormed out of the house with a gun, had upset her greatly. She wished she could make amends for him … maybe someday. "What are you and Maria up to?"

"Working hard, Helen. Trying to get a new collection together as fast as we can. The owner of The Working Girl shop in Seattle is ready to put a display in the window and Nordstrom's has shown some interest. Trouble is the commuting is taking up time, and Maria may soon be living in Seattle. A realtor called me about an apartment that would make a wonderful live-in studio but I just don't think I can swing it."

"My, my, so much you're taking on. Is this apartment available?" Helen asked adding a sugar cube to her tea.

"It is now, but I don't know for how long." Gilly leaned forward her forearms on the table.

With the look of a cat that was about to lay a prize mouse in front of Gilly, Helen cocked her head, looked over at the display of china cups and saucers, her lips slowly turning up. "You know, dear, I've been waiting for the right time to help you along and I have a proposition. I guess you could say a business proposition." She grinned as the girls' heads snapped up. What was Helen thinking?

"How much is the rent on this apartment?"

"$1100 a month." Gilly held her breath.

"Oh my, that's doable. Yes, very doable. How about I loan you the monthly rent for the first six months … give you a chance to get your collection ready and in front of potential buyers. In that time I would think you might have a few sales, and you'd be on your way. If you need a little extension, another month or so, you could let me know."

Gilly's hand again shot out grabbing Maria's arm. Did Helen just offer to loan her the money for an apartment? Seed money to start her business?

"Helen, I'm not going to let you think about what you just said. I accept your offer. I'll have my attorney write up an agreement." Smiling at Maria, she added, "I think my attorney could have that ready by tomorrow, don't you, Maria?"

"I'm sure of it."

"Oh, this is so exciting," Helen said beaming. "I was talking to my husband just last night about you. 'Loan them some money,' he said. His very words. 'All new startups need an angel to help them along.'"

Gilly jumped up and kissed both of Helen's rosy cheeks. "He's right. You are my angel. My lifesaver. It would take me months to build adequate funds to make the move. Helen, this means *Gillianne Wilder Fashions* is a giant step closer thanks to you."

Leaving the tearoom, Gilly gave her mom a kiss and said she see her at dinner. Anne noticed that whatever Gilly wanted to tell her suddenly didn't seem so bad. She and Maria strode out to the car a renewed spring in their steps.

~ ~ ~

Chicken potpies in individual ramekins, a tossed salad, and buttermilk biscuits were on the dinner table as the Wilder family sat down to eat.

"Dig in everyone before the pies get cold," Anne said picking up her fork.

"Looks mighty good, Anne," Gramps said. "Of course these biscuits are going to raise havoc with my waistline."

"What waistline is that, Dad?" Will chuckled as he reached for the blue-cheese salad dressing.

"So, Gilly, you said this afternoon that you wanted to talk to your dad and me. I presume that includes your grandfather."

"Of course." She looked at Gramps catching his wink although a knot suddenly gripped her stomach. "So much has happened the last twenty-four hours … I'm not sure where to begin."

"I suggest you stop playing with that piece of chicken and start from the beginning," Will said picking up another biscuit.

"Okay. There are really three things." Gilly looked at her family. They're not going to be happy about any of this, she thought. There's no easy way to tell them.

"A package came in the mail yesterday, here, addressed to me." Gilly walked to the dryer, opened her tote and pulled out the zippered plastic bag. She set it on the table between her mom and dad.

"What's in the box?" Will asked.

"Go ahead, open it, son." Gramps gave a reassuring pat on Gilly's shoulder.

Anne opened the bag and handed the box to her husband. "The brown paper is postmarked Paris?" She looked up at Gilly who was holding her breath watching her father lift the lid.

"That Goddamn son of a bitch," he snapped.

"Oh, Gilly, no!"

"Yes, Mom, another spike. There's more. Dad, please, you and mom, read the note." Gramps gripped her hand tight as they both watched for their reaction.

Will's lips tightened, his eyes closing to mere slits as his brow furrowed. "You lied to us. The father isn't dead and this son of a bitch is blackmailing you."

Anne closed her eyes, leaned back, unable to look at her daughter.

Will shoved the box, the note, and the brown paper back in the bag, yanked the zipper shutting the bag. "Is it true?"

"Yes, I loved—"

"Loved? You know nothing about love. You go traipsing off to Paris, without our blessing, and come back pregnant. Spare us the rest. That's all I need to know." Will got up and poured a shot of bourbon into a highball glass. He leaned against the refrigerator, sipped his drink, as Anne robotically cleared the dinner table. "So, what are you going to do about this, this letter?" he asked.

"I talked to Hawk this morning and he said I have to go to the police. He suggested Detective DuBois. He's the detective Skip followed during the investigation of the gold robbery—when Gramps found the key—"

"I know about the key. I'm asking you what *you're* going to do. So far you've said you're going to the police."

"Will, give her a chance," Anne said. Standing behind her daughter's chair, she gently kissed the top of her head, stroked her hair, and then sat down.

"That's it ... as far as the detective goes. I don't know what he'll say." Gilly went to the stove, poured boiling water over a teabag, nodded to Gramps asking if he wanted a cup. He nodded he would.

"Gilly, you said there was more you had to tell us," Anne said with a sigh.

"When Maria and I had lunch at the tearoom today, you saw Helen Churchill come in and sit with us?"

"Yes, but what—"

"She offered me a loan—a loan to pay the rent for an apartment in Seattle that will double as a studio to start—"

"My God, Gilly, out of the blue this woman offers to pay your rent? In Seattle?"

"It wasn't exactly out of the blue, Dad. She asked what I was doing and I mentioned to her that I had a couple of requests for samples, and one thing led to another, and that the commuting was becoming a problem but I didn't have enough money to pay rent *and* start my business, and she—"

"And she jumped at the chance to throw her money around?"

"Not exactly. She felt bad about the incident with Spiky, ah, her grandson, and Gramps having to shoot at him to scare him away. She said she had been trying to come up with a way to make amends ... and ... so, this is her way."

"Gilly, are you saying you're going to move to Seattle?" Anne asked turning to face her daughter to see if Gilly meant what she was saying but knowing she meant every word.

"Yes, Mom, but it's not far ... just across the sound."

"But the baby. How?"

"You did it, Mom. You had me. Took me to work with you—there are pictures of me in a ... in a basket."

Chapter 32

Gilly was relieved her parents knew the real story about the baby's father. Before they left for Port Gamble, her father brought his temper under control and even volunteered to go with her to see DuBois—putting his arms around her signaling a truce. She thanked him but said Skip would accompany her. Of course, she didn't let on that she hadn't asked Skip yet. Ready to leave, her mom had jumped out of the car telling her she'd bring her chicken potpies if she lived in Seattle or Victoria, Canada. Laughing, they wrapped their arms around each other one more time both wiping a tear away.

She loved her parents. They always seemed to rally around her no matter what she threw at them, but last night was a little over the top she had to admit. Her mom had whispered that her dad was excited over the prospect of a grandchild. Not so much about her plans to move to the city.

There was so much to do in Seattle today. Thankfully the forecast for rain proved to be wrong. The day had dawned bright and sunny. After Helen's bombshell that she would loan the money needed to rent an apartment, Gilly had called the realtor arranging an appointment to see the place. She also called her obstetrician for a referral to a doctor in Seattle. That was another appointment. But the most important item on her mind was the call she had put off. Skip.

Popping the morning vitamin tablet into her mouth she finished her glass of milk and went outside. Strolling to the front of the house she sat on the top step of the rickety stairs leading down to the beach and punched a number on her cell. Shading her eyes from the sun's rays bouncing off the water, she listened to the ring of Skip's cell.

"Skip Hunter."
"Hi ... it's Gilly."
Silence.

"I know. I haven't forgotten your voice," he said in a low husky voice.

Silence.

Tension transmitted one to the other.

"What's up?"

"I'd like to see you … today if possible. I have to talk to you … and I need a number for Detective DuBois."

She caught him off guard with that one. "That's a strange request."

"Can you meet me today? Can you meet me at the ferry terminal? I'm about to leave the house so I can just make the nine o'clock."

"Okay, the terminal. Are you all right? You sound … different."

"I'll explain when I see you."

~ ~ ~

Skip's heart pumped out of control when he saw her walking toward him at the main entrance inside the ferry terminal. She looked beautiful. Her hair had grown several inches over the last year falling in soft waves around her shoulders. She always garnered furtive peeks from passersby. Today was no exception. Even though she looked under control he still saw her as vulnerable. Damn it, he wanted to take her in his arms but there were too many walls blocking him to make a move. He jammed his hands in his pockets to keep from reaching out.

Seeing him she smiled but her eyes avoided his. He wondered if she was ever going to look at him again the way she had before she left for Paris. He knew she cared for him but how much? That was the question. He sure as heck loved her but stupidly hadn't said so. And now look. She was pregnant with another man's child. He didn't buy her story but … maybe in time. This morning he had to be content that she had called him for his help, whatever that may be. At least his bad behavior when he last saw her—accused her, for God's sake, of being pregnant hadn't stopped her from calling him. She needed him. Maybe he could build on that little crumb.

Clouds had rolled in and rain was beginning to puddle on the sidewalks. "Do you want me to get the car … or run to the café down the street? Where do you want to talk?" Skip asked.

"How about that bench over there? Most of the foot passengers are heading to the pier for the return ferry."

He followed her to the bench. She set her large tote beside her and turned to him. Looking square into his eyes, she said, "I'm in trouble."

"The baby? Is something wrong with the baby?" Without realizing it he had reached for her hand.

"The baby's fine."

"You?"

"Fine." Hesitating, she inhaled and plunged on. "I didn't tell you the truth about the baby's father. He's not dead. He's very much alive. Running for the Senate in France and he's also married." She looked down at Skip's hand. So strong. She didn't realize she was gripping his hand in return—her lifeline to … to what? She wondered if he would pull away but he hadn't so far.

"I met him shortly after I arrived in Paris. We started dating immediately. One thing led to another. I guess it was the classic tale of a stupid girl swept off her feet by a wealthy man. Skip, I thought he loved me. I thought I loved him. But I know now what I felt had nothing to do with love. I didn't really know him … oh, I thought I did. But I was so naive. I never checked him out, never questioned his advances."

"How old is he?"

"Mid-thirties, at least that's what he said."

"He took advantage of you, Gilly. My God, you didn't have a chance." Skip looked down, her hand was so small in his. He strengthened his grip. "What did he say about the baby."

"He doesn't know. I was going to tell him at our Friday-night dinner—"

"Friday night dinner?"

Gilly couldn't look into his eyes. She turned away. "Yes. Every Friday night. His wife … must have had a standing engagement so he had no problem seeing me."

Skip touched her chin, turned her face back to him. "The baby?"

"Before I could say anything he told me he had reconciled with his wife. She was going to stand by him because he was going to run for office in the French government. He was sorry. Hoped I would understand. I knew instantly how naive I'd been … too late. I got up, said goodbye, and left him standing in the restaurant."

Skip shook his head. Closed his eyes lifting her hand to his lips. Setting her hand back in her lap, he looked up. "That's when you concocted the story about the father being dead?"

"Yes. When I got back to my apartment my roommates were waiting. They helped me put together the story. Three weeks later I returned to Seattle."

"Did you see him again ... after ... after that night?"

"No."

"Gilly, thank you for telling me the truth. I take it you're not going to have an abortion. It's going to be hard ... a single—" The word caught in his throat.

"Oh, Skip, my baby ... the trouble I'm in isn't—"

Pulling her hand from his she opened her tote retrieving the plastic bag with the box, the wrapping paper, and the letter. "Two days ago I came home from a day in Seattle to find this on the kitchen table. Gramps said he found it in the mailbox a few hours earlier." Gilly's hand shook so hard she dropped the bag in Skip's lap.

He took the box out of the bag and opened it, recognizing the heart pierced with the spike, the identical heart and spike that the waiter had given Gilly from an unknown man that night when the family was having dinner at the Space Needle. A celebratory dinner for her winning the state-wide design competition.

Wincing, he shot her a glance, noticed the wrapping had a Paris postmark, and opened the letter. He looked at her for permission to read it. She nodded.

His face changed as he read. It had been soft and warm at seeing her. Now his expression was much like her father's when he read the letter—brow furrowed, cheeks and lips drawn tight. He refolded the paper and returned everything to the plastic bag. Reaching for his cell, he fingered through its directory and punched an entry.

"DuBois, please." Waiting for the call to go through he again picked up Gilly's hand. "Hi, Mirage. Skip here. You remember Gillianne Wilder? Clay Wilder's granddaughter? Yeah, that's right, the two who found the key to the gold, so to speak. Ms. Wilder is here with me and she needs to see you. She's received a blackmail letter and I think you'd better take a look at it. She could be in danger."

Chapter 33

Paris

Count Beaumont paced over the sumptuous Persian carpet in his library—right fist pounding his left palm. How could Maxime have done such a thing? And with an American tart. The Count had groomed his son for government office, the ruling class. And now this potential scandal could blast all his efforts to smithereens. Maxime was supposedly sterile. He and Bernadette never conceived a child. This harlot from the States must be lying. It couldn't have been Maxime—impossible he was the father of this woman's baby.

Maxime sat watching his father pace the room. He was understandably upset. He only hoped his father wouldn't banish him from the family. He rather liked his lifestyle. He had done everything his father asked of him, his mother had asked of him. They owed him.

"Maxime, I don't know how this Edward Churchill came to the conclusion that you fathered this child. For God's sake, you and Bernadette, ten years, nothing. This couldn't have come at a worse time. Even a hint of scandal with the election only a few months away could cause you to lose. Bernadette will certainly back out of the reconciliation."

Count Beaumont whirled, his eyes shooting daggers at his son. "Maxime, is this bastard child that Churchill is threatening to expose, is it possible you *are* the father?"

Maxime could tell lies without batting an eye but not to his father. Never. The man always saw through him, even when he was a little boy and snatched a cookie. He'd never been able to deceive the elder Beaumont. For the most part, once Maxime had become a man, his father had looked the other way never questioning his dalliances. After all his parents had practically arranged his marriage and once

Bernadette got what she wanted—access to the Beaumont fortune, she had turned cold, shrill, banishing her husband from their bedroom. It was no wonder he found relief in the arms of others. It had always been thought it was Maxime who couldn't father a child. None of his other conquests had become pregnant.

"Maybe this woman set you up. Maybe Edward Churchill is the father and the two of them are conspiring to bring you down if you don't pay them."

Maxime said nothing. It was always better to let his father rant. He was coming up with some interesting conclusions, but deep down Maxime knew it was very possible Gillianne Wilder's baby was his.

His father stopped in his tracks, turned and strode to his son. "We have to verify this information. First, you go see the doctor. Go to two doctors—compare their conclusions. If there is one drop of semen with adequate sperm to father a child if the woman is capable, I want to know about it. And, what are the odds? You tell this Churchill that his blackmail will not work—you are not the father. A loose woman could have dozens of men, anyone could be the father. Maybe he made the whole thing up. Thought the Beaumont's were an easy mark. Maybe he's bluffing. String him along."

The Count stomped to the sideboard, poured himself a crystal balloon of Brandy. Tossed it down, poured another and whirled again on Maxime. "Did you by any chance use a different name when you had your little fling? At a hotel, or wherever you stayed?"

"No—I didn't think it necessary. She trusted me—it was only a few short days in Milan. I didn't think she'd agree to stay with me if she thought there was a chance she'd—"

"Maxime, you didn't think. Period!" he shouted. "Bernadette will be so upset, she might well sell the story to the tabloid herself if she learns of it—blackmail the two of us to keep it quiet. No wonder she never agreed to fertility tests—maybe she was the one incapable of having children."

He helped himself to another brandy. "I'll get in touch with a detective, a very discrete detective, to go to Seattle. Nose around. Find out if the woman is indeed pregnant. We can't let even a hint of this come to light—if true. We must stop it, and you know exactly what I'm talking about."

Bernadette had escaped the dull conversation with her mother-in-law and had marched down the hall to find her husband. Hearing Count Beaumont shouting at Maxime, she pulled her hand back from the doorknob, listened. What had stirred up the old buzzard? Maxime fathered a baby? She had wanted a baby to secure her right to his money for as long as she lived. Her frozen heart turned to stone. Her disdain for her husband turned to hatred.

The shouting stopped.

Bernadette held her head up high. She would play the role of the reconciled, loving wife, until she found out if the words she had just heard were to be believed. If her husband had fathered a child, the possibilities of what she could do with the information were infinite.

Bernadette called to her husband as she opened the door to Count Beaumont's library. "Maxime. Maxime darling, your press secretary called. Something about a dinner tonight. A fund raiser. We must go home and change," she said with a smile. "She said the October air is a bit chilly. I believe it calls for my long mink. Don't you?"

Chapter 34

Seattle

An emotional roller coaster!

That's what Gilly climbed aboard every morning. Was she going to ride up, down, or slide sideways around a corner?

The meeting with Detective DuBois had been unsettling. He took the bag of *evidence* but so many fingers had handled the box, the brown wrapper, and the note that he doubted it would yield any clues as to the location of Edward Churchill, or as Gilly called him, Spiky. Given the postmark, he sent Churchill's picture and background to his counterpart in Paris—Detective Boisot. DuBois promised Gilly he'd alert detectives at the NYPD as well as issue an APB to his officers in case the guy returned to Seattle.

DuBois told her to keep her eyes peeled when she was out and to let him know if Churchill contacted her again. Other than that, it was a wait-and-see game. A game she did not want to play.

Skip had dropped her off at the realtor for her appointment to check out the apartment. Seeing Skip, confessing she had lied, and then telling him the true story, going with her to see DuBois, being protective—well, that sent her emotions up and down. When he asked if they could meet for dinner before she took the ferry back to Hansville she had declined.

He looked hurt. She was afraid of her emotions and pulled away from him again. The last thing she wanted to deal with was a relationship. Much better to keep her mind on her business and the responsibility she was carrying.

The apartment was perfect.

The coaster roared up.

She signed a short-term lease, put down the deposit, and made arrangements for Maria to pick up the key on November first.

The coaster soared to new heights when she called Nicole about some fabric. The conversation ended an hour later with a joyous, excited Nicole saying she'd be her second employee and to expect her within two weeks after Gilly and Maria moved into the apartment, a.k.a. her design studio.

~ ~ ~

To say the previous two weeks were hectic was an understatement. Suddenly it was November second.

Hallelujah, moving day!

Gilly, her mom and dad and Gramps, along with Maria and Hawk, had packed up the guesthouse studio the day before, plus all of Gilly's clothes that fit, and the maternity outfits her mom insisted on buying for her, as well as the items crammed into the bathroom cupboards and medicine cabinet.

They pulled out of Gramps driveway at sunrise, forming a convoy from Hansville to the Bainbridge ferry. After relaxing an hour on the ferry they once again formed the convoy snaking through the side streets of Seattle to Gilly's apartment.

The good news: it was only two miles from the Working Girl shop in the heart of Seattle's retail district. The bad news: the apartment was on the second floor.

Gilly stood her post in the apartment at her mother's insistence directing where everything was to go like a drill sergeant. Decorating didn't make the to-do list: all white walls, all beige carpeting except for the kitchen and bathroom covered in beige linoleum. Beige draw drapes came with the unit.

Learning how to cope with the cramped quarters in the Paris apartment she had shared with Nicole and Sheridan, she assigned one of the two very small bedrooms: one for sleeping, the other for clothes and the essential paraphernalia each girl couldn't live without.

The dining room and living room, designated as the studio, were quickly filled with bolts of fabric, a cutting table, and an additional folding table on which Maria's, Gilly's and her mom's sewing machines were set side-by-side. Her mom's for Nicole to use in case of an emergency sewing marathon.

Coco was the last to take up residence. Springing from her carrier she darted under a futon that Maria's mom and stepfather dropped off. They also contributed a slightly scratched small square table with three straight chairs, green, and a second dresser. Maria whispered to Gilly that she thought her stepfather was happy to have her out of the house, and permanently after she married Hawk.

Anne had packed a set of dishes, and Gramps surprised her with a microwave and a few pans. A set of utensils was put on a list along with kitchen gadgets. A can opener was essential.

The bunk beds were resurrected from Gramp's garage and he and Will reassembled them in the sleeping bedroom—Gilly now on the bottom bunk and Maria on top. Anne made up the beds with the sheets, blankets, and pillows the girls had used on the bunks in Hansville.

While Maria and, Hawk, Will and Gramps completed the unpacking, Anne and her daughter walked the two blocks to Gilly's new doctor. They expected to learn the sex of the baby she was carrying. Gilly checked in with the office attendant standing behind a sliding glass window. She handed Gilly a clipboard with several forms to be filled out before going in for her examination. Without hesitating, she answered the first question.

Father: deceased.

Removing her health insurance card from her wallet, she filled in the policy number. Thank goodness her mom and dad had insisted on taking out a policy when she began commuting to Seattle, the Design Academy, over a year ago. Checking off the remaining boxes making up her health history, Gilly handed the form back to the woman behind the glass and was soon called in to see the doctor—Dr. Sylvia Kirkpatrick.

The appointment proved to be routine, the doctor going over what Gilly could expect as the pregnancy moved into the final trimester.

"I'll see you next month, Gilly. Betsy, our technician, will be right in for your ultra sound."

"Thank you, Doctor."

The door to the examining room opened and the ultrasound technician came in. She was dressed in a brilliant white topcoat, a contrast to the short black curls swirling around her head. She carried a chart and her mouth was bowed into a pleasant smile.

"Hi, Mrs. Wilder. My name is Betsy. How are you feeling today?" she asked, as she pulled the equipment with the monitor a little closer to the examining table.

"Fine, thank you. This is my mom, Anne Wilder."

"Hello, Anne. How nice you're here to share this moment with your daughter. There is a chance we won't be able to tell for certain if it's a boy or a girl. A lot depends on the position of the baby. A little guy may not be ready to show himself," Betsy said with a chuckle.

She draped a sheet up under Gilly's chin then opened the gown leaving only her belly exposed. "I'm going to spread a conducting gel on your belly. It will feel a little cold at first, but then warms to your body temperature quickly. When the gel is in place I'll move a wand-like instrument across it. The wand emits high frequency sound waves which penetrate through the gel and your skin. As the sound waves penetrate various body parts, they are relayed to the ultrasound machine which constructs the images you will see."

"How long will this take, Betsy," Gilly asked turning her head to the monitor, but at the moment the screen appeared snowy.

"Oh, I imagine you will be up and dressed in less than an hour. Here we go."

The static-filled screen slowly began to show fuzzy areas in different shades of gray. Betsy very slowly moved the wand over Gilly's belly from side to side and sweeping around.

"Gilly, there's your baby."

Gilly's eyes were trained on the monitor, Betsy's hand continued to slowly move the wand as the image developed.

"Unless I'm mistaken, you are going to have a baby girl. What do you think of that?"

Gilly turned her head from the monitor and looked up at her mom. Tears welled up and spilled over their lashes—tears trickling freely from the eyes of both smiling women.

"Well, I guess from your reaction that you're happy. Your doctor has to confirm my findings, but I think she will agree. Would you like me to print a picture for you?"

"Oh, yes. Please." Gilly said.

Betsy turned off the machine and wiped the gel off of Gilly's belly. "There you are, my dear," she said, helping Gilly sit up on the edge of the table. "Let me get the picture from the printer next door. I'll be right back."

Betsy returned with the printed picture of Gilly's baby and handed it to the smiling expectant mother.

"When will I hear something from Dr. Kirkpatrick … if everything looks normal?"

"She should be back to you with the results in a few days, and, yes, she can tell if the baby appears healthy. But I don't think you have anything to worry about. You can get dressed now. I hope you enjoy your day," Betsy said, helping Gilly off the table.

Gilly gave the woman a hug. "You will never know how happy you've made me. Thank you, Betsy."

Leaving the doctor's office, Anne wrapped her arms around Gilly in a tight embrace. "I'm sorry, sweetie, I'm just so thrilled. I'll be hugging you a lot. Just think…a baby girl!"

"Yes, Mom, a baby girl. A healthy baby girl. I'm so relieved. I would have welcomed a little boy but I admit I was praying for a girl." I want nothing to remind me of Maxime, she thought.

"Let's stop at the cute deli on your street," Anne said. "Pick up sandwiches and drinks for everyone. They should be starved by now."

"Good idea, unless they finished and went out for something already."

"Well, then you'll have food for that little refrigerator." Anne stopped, pulled Gilly into her arms briefly, and continued walking. "Gilly, I like your apartment. But I'm worried about you. With Maria getting married in a few weeks, you'll be alone. I think you should come home on the weekends and I'll come over a couple nights a week."

"Oh, I forgot to tell you with all the frantic packing. Nicole, one of my roommates in Paris, is coming, moving to Seattle. When I left Paris she said she'd love to help me start the business—launch my label. I called her about buying some fabric I had seen at one of the textile warehouses, and that I had just signed the lease on the apartment. I told her it was time for her to join me and she surprised me by saying she'd ship the bolt of wool and a trunk with her clothes. She even volunteered to sleep on a blowup mattress until Maria was married and moved out."

"I should have known you'd come up with something," Anne said handing the bag of sandwiches to Gilly while she paid and picked up the drinks. "I'm glad you won't be alone."

Only a few buildings away from Gilly's apartment, Anne stopped again. "Gilly, has that detective found Edward?"

Gilly knew everyone helping her move was thinking about Spiky, they just hadn't said anything to dampen the festive front they were putting up. They were all concerned about her.

"Not yet. Don't worry, Maria and I will be careful, and I'll call you as soon as I know he's been arrested."

Chapter 35

Activity in the little apartment accelerated to a frenzied pace with Nicole's arrival. Maria ran double time tending to wedding plans, sewing samples for display, and training her replacement at the spa.

Nicole hit the ground running anticipating supplies needed for the break-neck speed of the collection and the sourcing of patternmaking, cutting and sewing factories to fill initial orders. She dangled a carrot in front of the representative of the factory she was considering for the first garments: if their workmanship proved to be up to her high standards, they would receive a contract as sales picked up. Nicole was a tough taskmaster warning the manager that if the patterns had errors, or the final garment wasn't acceptable because of flaws, she would demand they create the item again.

Anne maintained a schedule of an every-other-day trip from Port Gamble to Hansville to Seattle making sure Gramps *and* the girls in the fledging business were fed, especially ensuring that Gilly was eating properly.

Anne arrived at 11:30 Saturday morning with the weekend's meals and insisted everyone take a break for lunch. Gilly sat back in her folding chair, glass of milk in hand, and grinned at Maria and Nicole.

"I'm calling a staff meeting right now," she chuckled. Reaching into the basket in the center of the table she handed out notepads and pens as well as pulling a folder with a sheaf of papers out of her tote.

Nicole and Maria dropped into their matching, black metal folding chairs and looked at Gilly. It felt good to suddenly sit, let muscles relax and to breathe normally.

Gilly took another sip of milk tapping the top piece of paper full of notes with her pen. "We're playing catch-up because we jumped into the business outside of the normal season. We're behind the eight ball, heck, we haven't even chalked our cue stick."

How lucky am I to have such wonderful friends, she thought. Besides their support I think they actually believe in me. And my mom is pitching in from cooking to keeping the books. I only hope we can enter some numbers on the income side of the ledger soon.

"I've never played billiards," Maria grinned.

"Neither have I," Gilly said grinning back. "Anyway, I do have a plan, a set of objectives. We could have waited to set up our studio, but waiting meant loss of time and I could just see the savings I had put away to start the business begin to melt away. Of course there's my baby, and Maria's wedding. Nicole, thank God you joined us."

"I'm glad I did, too," Nicole said. "Starting a business is very exciting. Something I never would have had the nerve to do on my own."

"I second that," Maria added.

Gilly laid a clean sheet of paper on top of her folder and wrote: Gillianne Wilder Fashions.

"We start with a very targeted market—the career woman. *And* we start with five looks built around what I'll call the Suit-Dress, the key piece being the jacket. The jacket will mix and match with not only the dress, but pants, and a skirt. Initially, each look will be limited to three colors, and three sizes. Distribution to Nordstrom's and the Working Girl is considered ready-made—no alterations. But, a big *but*, we must constantly be on the lookout for wholesale opportunities—a great way to launch a label to hundreds of stores."

"Oh, Gilly, how in the world can we expect to do that?" Nicole asked.

"Events. Renting a stall, talking to consumers who attend, but also trying to catch the attention of wholesale buyers. Catching that buyer is a wildcard. Here's a list." Gilly shuffled through the papers to three yellow sheets detailing the upcoming events scheduled for January through April.

"Because there are only three of us to market this *breakout* collection," she smiled, "Each of us will wear multiple hats until we can afford to bring on staff as we grow. A dedicated salesperson will probably be the next employee." With a twinkle in her eye, she looked at Nicole. "I have an idea who that might be but we need a few sales first. I'm considering Gabrielle Dupont. What do you think, Nicole?"

"Gabby would be terrific. She was our agent, Maria. Late thirties, organized, and sales ability bar none. After all she placed Gilly and I, a couple of green beans, in jobs at prestigious fashion houses."

"Nicole, you've witnessed the designer's operations in Paris first hand. As you've already begun, you're in charge of sourcing the factories, overseeing their operation and making sure they understand that quality-of-work is paramount. Is that okay with you?"

"Yes, and I must tell you I'm very impressed with one factory in particular that I met with yesterday. They can handle patternmaking and sizing, moving to the cutting workroom, and then finally to the sewing workroom. And the manager, Mr. Tony Vinsenso, understands our urgency when the first orders come in but never at the cost of quality. He said he's ready to accept the orders. 'Bring it on,' he said. Actually I think he's rather intrigued about your starting a new label in Seattle. He sees Seattle as a potential rival to New York."

"Nicole, he isn't running a sweatshop is he?" Gilly asked concern crossing her face.

"No, no. He's very nice, businesslike, and very handsome."

"Oh, great. Just what we need. A handsome Italian." Maria said prompting a round of chuckles.

"Maria, the lookbook is beautiful," Gilly said. "All the descriptions and the position of the placeholders for the photos of the garments are perfect. I think by tomorrow morning we'll have finished the main pieces for the five looks. You can take them to the photographer but I want to go with you. It's very important that the models strike the right pose and I want to see the background. What do you think of white? Then you drop in other elements with your computer."

"I agree. I was hoping you'd come with me."

"Order three books. We'll print more as we make changes. *Then* after Nordstrom's and the Working Girl set up our display hopefully we'll see a few sales."

"Oh, you're going to have sales," Maria said. "I spoke with Susan Adams at Nordstrom's, and she said she already has a waiting list triggered by your designs in the competition."

Gilly closed her eyes, sighed, and snapped them open over a big grin. "This is exciting, isn't it?"

"Oh, yeah," Maria whispered.

"I like your label. It establishes your brand." Nicole said. "Gillianne Wilder Fashions."

"The URL for the website is www.GillianneWilderFashions.com," Maria said. "It will appear on all of our print material. Gilly, what about our titles on the business cards?"

"No titles. Only names for now, the website, and include cell-phone numbers. Limit the print run as I'm sure there will be changes. Maybe print two hundred with each of our names and the company name. And add *Designs for the Career Woman* under the company name: Gillianne Wilder Fashions."

"What about a street address?" Maria asked.

"I've been struggling with that. A post office box sounds so temporary, fly-by-night. Use our street address. The apartment is in my name so mail or deliveries should not be a problem. How about the word *Studio* after the company name followed by the street address, city, etcetera?"

"Good. I'll update the computer files." Maria said jotting the added task to her list.

Anne walked through with a cup of coffee and a notebook. "Don't forget, I'm keeping the books. Make that the chief cook, bottle washer, and bookkeeper. Someone has to keep you girls in line—three designers in one apartment will keep me busy I'm sure.

"You got that right, Anne," Maria called out. "You're the best at that chief cook thing. You deserve a medal."

"Gilly, how soon can we get into rhythm with the design seasons? We should be preparing for February shows with next year's fall collection. Are we going to show a new fall collection on the runway?"

"I think we need a year's fashion calendar—January through March to show fall and winter; July through October to show spring and summer—to learn the ropes, but as I mentioned earlier, there are a few consumer shows already on the calendar here in Seattle. The conventional wisdom is not to spend a lot of money on the display but to do everything tastefully—simple but eye-catching. Maria I think that falls under your marketing hat. Some designers I've spoken with felt it was a great way to launch a new line but to go into the event with the idea of getting feedback from buyers who stop at the booth. The point for us at this stage is to build a set of valuable contacts and to collect information both from potential buyers as well as actual consumers who stop to chat and maybe land some sales."

"So, our goal is to make sales in the coming months while quietly launching the line," Nicole said. "And we can perform market analysis by attending consumer events throughout the year."

"That's right. Perhaps at a late summer or early fall event we'll introduce our spring collection. That should put us on track to attend a fashion week here on the west coast, maybe California, or here in Seattle a year from now. All our efforts for this first year are to launch the label, gain market awareness, hopefully obtain a couple of endorsements, and try to break even. Of course, if all that comes true we will have outgrown this apartment serving as our studio."

"Whew. That's some plan," Maria said. "I need another cup of coffee."

"Wait, that's not all. We want to be on the lookout for space to open our own store—a small, sophisticated boutique-like place to meet buyers in a setting to show off our label and the essence behind GW Fashions. One guest speaker at school said it can help a new company to show the brand concept in a compact space. But that's hard to pull off as a startup. Money, money, money. However ... we should be on the lookout."

"By the way, Nicole, ask that factory manager you like, Mr. Vinsenso, what he can offer us in the way of sourcing current fabrics and trimmings at a good price. We've chosen unique fabrics for our first five looks true to our concept—wrinkle free, soft draping. The fabric I asked you to buy in Paris is an example, but the more Vinsenso can help the better."

Marie looked up from her notes. *"Gillianne Wilder provides the highest quality designs for the career woman's go-to wardrobe."*

Gilly laughed. "Trying out your marketing elevator statement on us?"

"You bet," Maria said. "I want all of our print materials to hype who we are and what our label stands for."

The buzzer sounded. Anne trotted down the stairs to see who was at the door. A few minutes later she returned with a package addressed to Gillianne Wilder, marked *Open by addressee only.*

Gilly froze. She recognized the handwriting. It was postmarked Tacoma, Washington. She reached into her tote for the pair of examination gloves DuBois gave her and pulled them on. She then slit the plastic tape sealing the small box and opened it. It contained a red heart with a steel spike identical to the others. Everyone knew the story about Edward Churchill and a chill swept over the room. The excitement of launching the new line evaporated.

Gilly pulled out the folded piece of paper under the heart and read the type-written message.

"Hello, Bitch.

As promised, here are the instructions for the payment you owe me as stated in my previous correspondence. You are to wire $20,000 to the account number below within seven days. If you do not, well, Paris will be a twitter with yet another scandal. Do not try to find me. It's rather amusing to change my name almost every day, and the bank account is secret. Spiky."

A long number followed with instructions to complete the wire transfer.

Gilly refolded the letter and put everything in a zippered plastic bag. "I guess this ends our staff meeting. I have to go see Detective DuBois." Gilly kissed her mom and slipped on her coat. "You'll be gone before I get back, Mom. Thanks for your help. The sandwiches were terrific and I can smell the beef stew in the pot. Take care, guys. I'll be back as soon as I can."

Gilly darted out of the apartment averting her eyes so they couldn't see how much the package had upset her.

Chapter 36

Ducking into the deli around the corner from her apartment, sleet rolling off her trench coat, Gilly stood behind the picture window steamed up around the edges framing a display of breads sticking out of baskets. She placed the call to Detective DuBois. He said he was on the road and would swing by to pick her up at the deli in ten minutes.

Gilly hesitated, clutching her cell, watching the sleet peck at the deli's window. Should she make a second call?

A month had slipped by since Skip had last escorted her to see DuBois. He hadn't phoned and she couldn't blame him. The touch of his hand on her elbow that day, guiding her out of the ferry terminal, had sent shock waves up her arm and smack into her heart. How did she respond? She had retreated behind a wall of indifference. So why call him now? Because he made her feel safe and at the moment she felt very vulnerable. She quickly punched his number before she second guessed her motive.

"Skip Hunter."

"Hi."

"Gilly … you okay?"

"A little shaky." Hearing his voice she felt sad and excited at the same time. Sad because she had betrayed him. Excited—the timber of his voice, she could almost feel him touching her cheek. "Dubois is picking me up in a few minutes. I received another package from Spiky. Instructions with the bank account. Where I'm supposed to wire the money."

"Is DuBois taking you to his office?"

"Yes."

"I'll meet you there. Maybe we can go out for a drink after, if you have time."

"Oh, I—"

"Oh … well, you can have a glass of milk and I'll have a beer."

Milk? A beer? They were going to be near each other—at least for more than a few minutes. "DuBois just drove up. See you at the police department." Gilly tossed her cell into her bag and darted out to the unmarked squad car sliding in away from the freezing rain before the detective had a chance to get out and open her door.

"I hope you don't mind, Detective, Skip Hunter is joining us."

"Not a problem. When did the package arrive?" DuBois pulled away from the curb merging with the traffic, the wipers swiping the windshield.

"About an hour ago. I used the special gloves you gave me—put the box and the letter in a plastic bag for you."

"Okay, this won't take long, then you and Hunter can be on your way." The detective stole a glance at his passenger. He saw a composed, tough woman sitting beside him. A woman who was becoming very pregnant. "When's your baby due?"

"End of March—I'm four months along and counting," she said. No smile. She stared at the sleet sluicing down the windshield. Apprehension had replaced a smile.

Entering his office, DuBois helped her off with her coat, gave it a shake, and hung it on the old wooden coat tree beside the door. Gilly smoothed down her shirt just as Skip walked through the door. Placing his hand on the small of her back, he leaned around her to shake hands with the detective. Inhaling a quick breath Gilly moved away and sat on a chair facing the detective's desk. Reaching across the desk she laid the zippered plastic bag in front of him.

DuBois pulled on a pair of latex examination gloves, handing a second pair to Skip. Both men read the letter. DuBois returned the items to the bag and called an officer from forensics to pick it up for testing.

"Spiky didn't give you any way to contact him," DuBois said looking at Gilly. "I suggest you do nothing. Wait for him to come back and ask for the money again. Meanwhile we'll step up the search for him, do some checking on that account number. Somehow he's tracking you. Sent that package to your Seattle address. You haven't been there very long."

"Only two weeks. His grandmother, Helen Churchill, knows the address. She's loaning me the rent money. For six months."

"Does she know about the blackmail?"

"No, only about when he assaulted me, and Gramps shooting at him. I think at first she was ambivalent about the incident, after all he is her grandson. But then she changed—obviously trying to support me. The rent maybe her way of making amends for what Edward did to me."

"I think I'll take a run out to Port Gamble," DuBois said. "Talk to her. Feel her out. See if she'd call us if he told her where he's hiding. I don't like the fact he's so blatantly taunting you. He's in your face and I want you to keep your guard up." DuBois said the last words looking straight at Skip."

DuBois obviously thinks I should be watching out for Gilly's welfare, Skip thought. How was he supposed to do that when she barely talked to him? But, she did call him today. Another start. Or ... another wall.

~ ~ ~

Skip took Gilly to Pike Place Market known for fresh produce stalls, souvenir boutiques as well as small shops with general merchandise, and a wide variety of restaurants. Holding her hand, he led her to Lowell's, dining rooms on three floors, all with a view of Puget Sound.

It was a restaurant, bar, and market displaying fresh fruit, vegetables and fish—lots of fish—a bright, cheerful place for a bite to eat and casual conversation and as far from romantic as you can get unless you visit at night when it's aglow with candles. He didn't want to stir up any tension where she might dart away—just friends getting together at the end of a day. Trouble was she looked so darn cute—white long-sleeve shirt over jeans, the baby bump now obvious. She certainly had enough to deal with and romance, he was sure, was not at the top of her list, or anywhere on the list.

"How's it going in your new place?"

"Great. Maria's staying with me."

"What happens when she gets married?"

"Oh, my staff is growing. There are three of us—four counting my mom. Nicole Bruni, my roommate from Paris—"

"Yeah, I met her," Skip blurted. Damn, why did I say that—another reminder of when she was away from me—way, way, away.

"Oh, yes ... I forgot." Gilly said with a sheepish smile guilt twisting her stomach in a knot. "When I left Paris Nicole told me she wanted to come to the States, said if I needed her help to ask. I called and she said yes. We're all working very hard and should be delivering the display samples in a couple of days to two stores. Mom is taking care of the books—hopefully we'll get some income as everything is out-go now." The knot eased and Gilly smiled at Skip. She wanted to put her hand out on the table, offering him a chance to respond. But she didn't. She kept her hands tightly clasped in her lap, except when she took a bite of the stuffed shrimp. Even though she had lunch a couple of hours earlier she was hungry again.

"Skip, have you been working on your novel? The expose of the Wellington gold robbery?"

"Yeah, but I'm stymied on the ending. I feel there's something more. I just feel that Eleanor Wellington had something to do with Sacco's death but the police can't find any evidence, and worse yet, no body. I wish I'd receive another phone call with one of those anonymous tips I got leading to Sacco in the first place."

"Ah, those bones of yours talking to you again—like you felt about the guy who was found lying in the surf by Gramp's house."

"Yeah, something like that."

"Can I read it ... sometime?"

Her request took his breath away. Such a simple request but he had poured his heart and soul into the manuscript, taking great pains to keep it accurate. He didn't want anyone to read it. Not yet. But Gilly wasn't anyone. He trusted her and she was part of the story. "Sure. Yeah. I'd like you to tell me what I can do to make it a good read."

"You're the writer. I doubt I can help with *the read*. I'm sure the book will be a page turner."

"So far that makes two of us—both biased. I've sent out a few query letters to agents."

"And?"

"And, no dice—'I only take completed manuscripts,' or 'we don't take new authors,' or 'not our genre.' It's depressing. I don't know ... maybe I just can't write, or I can't write what someone else wants to read."

"I do know your daily articles in the newspaper were riveting. Gramps saved them during the time I was away. I read them all. Don't give up. You're good. I bet Agatha Christie didn't stop with her first rejections. She kept writing. If in your heart you believe the ending hasn't appeared, then start another expose. I'm sure you have lots of subjects—the stories you bring to light everyday through your *investigative reporting*."

There it is, he thought. The sparkle, the enthusiasm of the young girl before she went to Paris. I'd like to be the one to keep that sparkle in her eyes.

"By the way, I like your new look—slight five-o'clock shadow matching a shadow of hair—very Hemingway." She unconsciously slid her hand out on the table. Quickly pulled back.

The action was not lost on Skip, but he made no move. "I was talking to Wellington a couple of days ago. His gold is being shipped back to him from Mexico where Eleanor and Sacco had squirreled the gold bars away. He flew down, opened every crate, and counted the bars. Out of the forty-five million I guess Eleanor only had time to spend a couple million," Skip chuckled. "DuBois, or rather the Mexican police detective he worked with, tracked the fence who sold some of the gold giving Eleanor money to spend. A little hard to buy a drink with a gold bar." Skip looked at Gilly sitting on the opposite side of the table. He wanted to knock the table away and pull her into his arms.

"Wellington is throwing a party in celebration once his gold is safely back in his possession. This time he's keeping it in a bank vault and not his house. I know he's going to ask your grandfather and you. Can I escort the two of you? It should be in a couple of weeks."

"Of course. Sounds fun and I'm sure Gramps would be thrilled to attend with you. Did you receive the invitation to Hawk and Maria's wedding? That's in three weeks, then it's Christmas. Time is flying."

"I did. Again, can I offer you a ride?"

"I'd like that, Skip. Thanks."

"Just let me know which side of the sound you're on—your apartment or Gramp's."

An awkward silence followed.

No more topics to discuss—no more safe topics.

He wanted to ask what he could do to help keep her safe. He wanted to move in with her but he didn't think that idea would fly either. He settled for driving her home, insisted on walking her to her door standing back until she disappeared into her apartment.

Chapter 37

It was a big day.

A big, big day!

The girls woke and padded on bare feet to their little kitchen. After their first sip of coffee, the three broke out in big smiles. Within two hours they would be delivering the display samples to Susan Adams at Nordstrom's and Stacy Sinclair at the Working Girl shop.

"Last one in the bathroom has to buy lunch," Nicole called out as she slipped away from the table, shut the bathroom door giggling.

"Hey, Bruni, you're not playing fair. You had a head start and our little mother can't run," Maria yelled laughing. "Five months down and four to go, girl friend."

"If I can't run now, I hope I can still get out of a chair by then."

Maria shook her head. "Can you believe it? *We* are delivering the first garments with the label, *Gillianne Wilder Fashions*."

"I know. I know. Thank God Hawk let you borrow his van. If we ever get Nicole out of the bathroom *and* get ourselves dressed we'll load up," Gilly said, throwing half of her coffee down the sink, refilling her mug with milk.

"Let me amend that statement," Maria said. "While you're in the bathroom, Nicole and I will load the van. You can sashay down the stairs or whatever it is you call you're waddle these days, and climb into the front seat. You're going to ride like a queen today, at least until we dress the mannequins. Susan said she'd set them up for us in the lady's department. Then *you* have to pay attention to every detail because I'll be too excited." Maria said as she headed for her little space in the bedroom dressing room to put on her jeans. When Gilly emerged from the bathroom, Nicole was carting down the last pieces of the collection.

The morning traffic was thick, but Maria was an expert at navigating the Seattle streets. A few blocks later she turned the van down the alley to Nordstrom's loading dock.

"Now, girl friend, you are not to lift a finger until Nicole and I have the pieces up in the lady's department and then only to adjust a scarf. Understood?" Maria turned off the engine of the van and held Gilly's eyes in a mock-stern face.

"Understood, but I can take that large tote with the tops. You get the jackets and the other pieces. Nicole, I love the garment bags. However did you get our logo printed so fast?"

"Oh, I just worked my Persian whiles on this cute guy at the graphic print shop," Nicole giggled, batting her long black lashes. "Do you realize this is the first time and maybe the last that we'll back up to a loading dock. Vinsenso will be doing all future honors."

In no time the garment bags were hanging on a rack the department manager had positioned next to the mannequins. "Look at that gold easel and framed poster would you," Maria said gaping as she read out loud. "Announcing *Gillianne Wilder Fashions* now available for pre-order. Gillianne Wilder, the winner of the State's fashion designer competition."

A chill of excitement passed through the three girls. "This is it. This is it! Your label is launched," Nicole said squeezing Gilly's arm.

Gilly wiped a tear off her beaming face. "Okay, you guys, let's get these naked ladies dressed. We have another store to visit." Gilly carefully slid the dress over the mannequin's head, topping it with a shimmery cropped jacket, the first of two looks. The second, the jacket was reversed, and topped a beautiful tank top over a pencil skirt.

Maria set a lookbook against the easel describing the various pieces: reversible two-in-one jacket—pants, sleeveless dress, and another top—the dress doubling as a party dress ready for ropes of gold, or pearls, or other gems. The lookbook listed the three sizes available, and three color palettes.

Arriving at the Working Girl shop, Nicole and Maria carted the three looks for the career woman in the garment bags. Stacy had placed three mannequins in the window under sheets waiting to be dressed with the new line. It didn't take Gilly long to add her finishing touches. Stacy and the girls hustled outside to admire the new window display. As with Nordstrom's, Stacy had prepared a sign in a shiny ebony frame announcing the new label.

"Let's go back inside," Stacy said. "I have something to tell you, to discuss."

Gilly felt a tense undercurrent from Stacy. She was not her usual spirited self. Stacy called to her salesgirl that she would be in the back if she was needed.

Sitting at a table, Gilly looked at Stacy. She was growing more apprehensive by the minute. "Is this good news or bad news?" she asked.

"Well, it depends. Good for me, something I've been ready to do for at least a year. And, an offer to you. But you may not be ready to take advantage of it."

"For heaven's sake, don't keep us in suspense," Maria said trying to be lighthearted but failing. She felt tension-filled vibes in the air.

"I'm going to retire. Sell the shop."

Her statement came out in a rush as if, had she not said it quickly, she might not say it at all.

"Oh, Stacy, you're not sick are you?" Gilly reached out for Stacy's hand.

"No, no. I'm fine. My husband retires in a few months and we want to do some traveling."

"You said something about an offer," Nicole whispered.

"Yes. Gilly, this is a prime spot. Perfect really for someone such as yourself, a new designer launching a label, a perfect place to test market your brand." Stacy's eyes began to twinkle. "I wonder if you want to manage the shop for six months adding your designs to the existing stock. I could help you with the transition to manager. Then if things go well, you could take over the lease and I'll sell you the business."

Gilly's jaw dropped. "I…I…don't know what to say." She looked from Stacy to Nicole to Maria. Her friends were as dumbfounded as she was. Their heads switching from one to the other and around again.

"You've never seen the second floor. There's an apartment and plenty of space for a design studio. I know it's sudden," Stacy continued. "But the more my husband and I discussed our plans, the more I thought about you, and how I started the shop. But I always sold other designer's clothes. You would have a retail outlet that wholesale buyers could visit, see your brand in a setting that you design to show off your label in the best light. Your light."

"I…I…"

"Think about it, dear. The holidays are upon us—Thanksgiving this week, Christmas just around the corner. I'll need your answer by

January first … a new beginning on the first day of the New Year. How does that sound, unless you don't want to consider the offer. Maybe too soon?"

"Of course, I want to consider it. I'm overwhelmed is all … and with your faith in my designs. I want Nicole and Maria and I to run out in the street, throw our Mary Tyler Moore hats in the air and scream YES! YES! YES!"

Chapter 38

The three girls plus Anne sat around the table eating turkey wraps slathered with cranberry chutney from the tearoom. A salmon casserole with peas and carrots was in the refrigerator, big enough Anne hoped that they could eke out two dinners.

The four were brainstorming if, or how, they could swing the takeover of the Working Girl shop along the guidelines that Stacy had laid out. The brainstorming was actually a continuation and refinement of the discussions that had ensued around the Thanksgiving table. Anne, Will, and Gramps had sprung for all the fixings prepared by the neighborhood deli.

Today's discussion, while spirited, was honing in on whether taking Stacy up on her offer was really doable—in other words the money angle.

"With the apartment included, we would be living relatively rent free for the first six months as we manage the shop," Gilly said. "That would give us a chance to bankroll Helen's rent money until we pick up the lease. Of course, the lease will triple the amount we're paying now. Stacy said she'd show us her books. But if she's paying the rent from her sales, then I don't see any reason why we can't."

"As I see it," Maria said. "It all depends on how many sales are generated from the display samples we dropped off last week. If there aren't very many, then I say we have to pass on the deal."

Gilly's cell rang, and as she answered she said, "I agree, Maria. Hello. ...Oh, Stacy, sorry I was just talking to Maria and Nicole. Your offer has us spinning. What's up?"

"I had to call, Gillianne Wilder." Whenever Stacy got excited she always called Gilly by her full name. "I've had several orders for your collection. Do you think you can deliver them by January second? They all said they wanted something new to spice up their wardrobe for the dreary winter months ahead."

"Yes. Sure we can deliver. That's wonderful. I'll be down in an hour to pick up the orders and get them off to our factory manager. Oops, I have another call. See you in about an hour, Stacy. Hello, Gillianne Wilder here. Oh, hi, Ms. Adams ... What? ... Wait a minute. You have some orders? Several orders?"

"Yes, Mrs. Wilder, on the condition they can have the clothes by January first or the day after being the first is a holiday. If not, they will cancel."

"Well, Ms. Adams, you tell them, yes. I'll drop by in an hour to pick up these orders and any others you write up. We'll get right on it. And, Ms. Adams, thank you."

Gilly hung up her eyes bulging, jaw dropping. Nicole, Maria and Anne looked back at Gilly all bug-eyed, and dropped jaws. Gilly screamed back: "Do you understand what just happened?"

"Yes, dear," Anne said. I'll help you pack so you can move into the Working Girl shop on January first."

Nicole started screaming, jumping up and down, skittering back and forth high-fiving everyone including Coco.

~ ~ ~

Gilly and Nicole put on their coats and Anne volunteered to drive them to the Working Girl shop on her way to the ferry. She was already making lists of what she had to do at home in order to be free to help her daughter. Maria said she'd take the opportunity to run some errands and buy a few items she needed for Hawk's new apartment, soon to be their apartment.

First stop was to pick up the orders from Stacy, and then Gilly and Nicole scooted over to Nordstrom's. Ms. Adams met them with a fist full of order sheets. Another five orders complete with style numbers, sizes, and colors, had come in. She handed the paperwork to Nicole and rushed off to help another customer.

Gilly and Nicole walked down the hill to the subway station chattering like magpies as Nicole read off the order sheets. Nicole jumped aboard the train, holding out her hand to help Gilly. They stepped off at their stop and walked the block to the main entrance of the factory. Tony Vinsenso greeted Nicole with a hug and shook Gilly's hand vigorously. Business had been a little slack and when he saw the orders in Nicole's hand as she shoved them at him, he hugged Gilly as well.

"Take a look, Tony, and I need copies before I leave." Nicole said. "Do you see any problems in filling the orders?"

"Only the fabric from Paris. Fortunately the bolt you brought here will suffice for these orders. My cutters and the girls on the sewing floor will be excited to have more work. I'll get on the phone right away to the textile factory in Paris and have several bolts shipped FedEx."

"You know, Mr. Vinsenso, while we want the orders to be in the stores by December thirtieth, superior workmanship must not be compromised. Please don't rush at the expense of quality. Nicole will drop by at least every other day to check," Gilly said.

"Don't you worry, Mrs. Wilder. When Vinsenso says he can deliver a quality garment on time, Vinsenso will deliver."

"Wonderful. Nicole I'm going to head back to the apartment while you go over every line item with him. I'll see you later. Thanks again, Mr. Vinsenso." Gilly shook his hand and headed back to the subway.

Standing on the station platform waiting for the next train, Gilly pulled a little notepad from her large tote to start yet another list. She heard the train and started to inch forward when she felt a sharp blow to her back pushing her forward.

Horrified, she saw the edge of the platform—she was falling onto the tracks of the oncoming engine.

Screaming, her arm flailed out but there was nothing to grasp but air.

Everything went black.

Opening her eyes, she tried to focus on the man standing over her. People were circling around, looking down at her.

A medic rushed up pushing the crowd aside.

Bending over, he asked if she was okay as he opened his case, promptly reading her pulse with a stethoscope the silver disk pushed to her wrist. Gilly knew her beat was erratic and she had a hard time focusing. Again he asked if she was okay.

"I … I think so. I … I almost fell in front of the train." She grasped her swollen belly, "My baby…"

"We'll take you to the Emergency Room … Mrs.—"

The other medic had her purse open. "There's a card here for a Skip Hunter at the Seattle Times. That you're husband?"

"I …"

"Don't try to talk. We'll call him. He can meet us at the hospital." The medic held the card and placed the call throwing her purse beside the gurney.

"But …"

Gilly felt herself being lifted onto the gurney and whisked away through the crowd. She was lifted into a van. It screeched from the curb, through the streets, the siren blaring. The van drew up to the emergency entrance of the Swedish Medical Center. Her gurney was lifted out, the wheels snapped down, then rolled through the sliding glass doors to a sterile white room.

A man, she presumed was a doctor, came in along with a nurse. The doctor muttered a few words to the nurse, she nodded and left. He poked and prodded looking to see her reaction, any indications that she felt pain. She didn't seem to.

Her head was throbbing and she closed her eyes. She felt a hand grasp hers and knew Skip was by her side.

"Mrs. Wilder, you certainly had a scare."

Fluttering her eyes open Gilly turned her head and was able to focus on the man in the white coat addressing her.

"Two things helped you avert a disaster. Your coat tangled with the wire on a trash container and a man grabbed your arm as you tumbled forward. He pulled you back, toppled over you just as the train pulled into the station. You have a nasty bump on your head from when you slammed into the pavement."

"My baby?"

"I think your baby's fine. No trauma around your belly. I want you to stay here for an hour–observation just to make sure. We'll put some ointment on those scratches on your knees and palms when you tried to break your fall. Then you're free to go home. Mr. Hunter here said he'd see you got home safely. If you should have any spotting in the next couple of days, be sure to see your obstetrician right away, probably a good idea to visit your doctor in any case, but I don't think you'll have any trouble. Here, let's get you sitting up on the edge of bed. Do you feel dizzy?"

"Maybe a little. But I can see better."

"As I said you have a nasty bump but from what the medics said when they brought you in, you didn't lose consciousness. Maybe for a few seconds when you sustained that bump. Take it easy for a couple of days."

"Thank you, Doctor. I will."

The doctor patted her on the shoulder, and hustled off to another patient. Skip crouched in front of Gilly, holding both of her hands. God, he thought, what would I do if I lost her?

"You sure you feel okay to walk?" he asked.

"Skip, someone pushed me," she whispered.

"What? Are you sure?"

"Yes. I didn't see him coming. The platform was very crowded. He couldn't have *run* into me. I felt a sharp elbow or fist hit my back. But no one said anything about my being pushed. No one said they saw someone but then the medics rushed me away. No one asked any questions. Skip, I think it was Edward. I swear I heard him say 'bitch' just like on the card."

"I'll talk to DuBois. He's going to Wellington's party tomorrow night, which, young lady, you are not attending."

"I beg your pardon, big brother. I *am* attending and if you're reneging on your offer to take me, I'll ask Maria to go with me."

"You redheads. Stubborn. Stubborn. Stubborn. We'll talk about it tomorrow. If you feel okay, then…"

"Then, you'll pick me up?"

"Yeah. I'll pick you up."

"Excuse me. Mrs. Wilder?"

A man, his right arm in a sling and a heavily bandaged hand sticking out of the end, took a tentative step into the doorway. One leg of his trousers was torn at the knee, his jacket rumpled over his free arm. Fortyish. His short black hair was disheveled.

Skip wheeled around, stepping in front of Gilly. "Who are you?"

"Arthur Lewis." The man tried to look around Skip at the same time Gilly pulled Skip's arm so she could see the man.

"I'm Ms. Wilder."

"Sorry to bother you, ma'am. I'm sorry I fell on you—hope I didn't hurt you."

"You're the man who pulled me back from the tracks?"

"Yes. I was reading the newspaper, want ads. Here, I think this is yours." The man pulled Gilly's purse out from under his jacket.

"But … how?"

"The medics. They took you so fast they didn't hear me. I tried to get their attention. They forgot your purse. Excuse me for squinting—my glasses broke."

"Mr. Lewis, have a seat. Please," Gilly said pushing Skip to get the man a chair.

Arthur Lewis sat down and looked up at Gilly sitting on the edge of the hospital bed.

She sighed and leveled her gaze at the man. "Mr. Lewis, I felt a sharp ... a punch in my back causing me to fall. Did you see—"

"Mrs. Wilder, a man bumped me just before you began falling, so I can't say yes or no. It was a blur to be honest with you."

"Your hand's bandaged ... and that sling ... what happened?" Skip asked leaning against the bed.

"Sprained the wrist when I tried to break my fall."

"You said you were reading the want ads. What do you do?" Gilly asked.

"I'm an accountant. Was an accountant. It seems nobody needs one these days."

Gilly mulled over what the man said for all of two seconds. "Well, I do. Not full time ... a few hours a week ... hopefully more soon. Want to take a crack at it?"

"I don't have my resume with me."

"You saved my life—two counting my baby. That's the best resume in my book."

"But you don't know if I can add two and two."

"Well, you returned my purse. Skip, is my wallet in there ... next pocket ...no, the other one."

Skip pulled out a wallet, waved it at her, his eyes bulging. What the heck was she doing?

"So, Arthur Lewis, you're honest. I guess you can learn two and two. If not, we'll part company." Gilly smiled sweetly at Skip who looked like he wanted to intercede big time. "Can you hand me one of my business cards? Center pocket."

Skip retrieved the card, handed it to her and pulled a pen out of his shirt pocket laying it in her outstretched hand with a slight bow.

"Thanks."

Another sweet smile.

""Here, Mr. Lewis, if you aren't employed by January second, and if you'd like a few hours a week, say, two full days, and if you don't mind working for a pregnant, red haired fashion designer, I'll see you at one o'clock—just a half day to get your feet wet. Here's the address. Ask for me." Gilly handed Arthur Lewis her card.

He stood tall, gave Gilly and Skip a hearty handshake and strutted out of the examination room.

"Okay, Mr. Reporter—you told the doctor you'd take me home. Let's go! I could use another aspirin."

Chapter 39

Paris

Count Beaumont, face red with rage, nostrils flaring with each breath, stared at the doctor's lab report lying in front of him. Maxime stood in front of his father's desk, head down wiping his sweaty palms on his handkerchief.

"Says here that you have enough sperm to impregnate a quarter of the women in France. One American would certainly not have been a problem for you." The senior Beaumont spit out the words through clenched teeth. He saw his world crumbling. The hours, the money he had spent on his son—the best schools, the best clubs, the best women and for what? So he could impregnate a foreigner, a commoner? No! It must not be. He needed his son in the Senate in order to pass legislation, laws favorable to his clients' legal battles. Because his son couldn't keep his pants zipped their worlds were in jeopardy.

He rose, stomped to the palladium window heavily draped with velvet, looked out at his vast estate—manicured flower beds and lawns, horses grazing in the fields beyond, a state-of-the-art barn and paddock.

He whirled around. Eyes narrowing.

"Tell me again the message this lunatic left on your answering service."

Maxime was a self-assured man, knew his way around the aristocracy, the government, his business contacts, and women, well, most women, but he withered when even in the shadow of his father. After all Maxime's lofty living standard was due to his father's wealth and his grandfather's before that. His wife, Bernadette, spent her allowance from one end, as Count Beaumont deposited funds in the front end. Maxime was caught in the middle.

"He was screaming," Maxime whined. "Must have been drunk. Sounded drunk. He threatened to kill me, Father, if the money was not deposited immediately. He screamed that he was in terrible pain, that he had to have the money for an operation."

The Count poured a stiff shot of scotch. "If he's in so much pain maybe he'll do away with himself," he muttered. He turned and snarled at Maxime. "Of course, you don't know who *he* is, don't know how to find him, so we'll never know if he's dead or alive. Wire $25,000 tomorrow. Maybe that will placate the bastard until we can get rid of the problem."

"I thought the *problem* would have been eliminated by now." Maxime slumped in a soft black leather chair and stared into the flames flickering in the stone fireplace—a fire that didn't warm the chill of winter but flared with the heated words of his father.

"Well, so did I," Beaumont said. "But it seems the woman is always surrounded by a fortress of people since her bungled accident at a subway station. My contact is pushing forward. He has a new plan. Fool proof he says. But he has to be careful because of her gaggle of protectors. Time is running out. If we don't resolve the situation before the baby is born then the operation becomes much more difficult."

Bernadette backed away from the library door, strode quickly back down the hall to her mother-in-law's sitting room. Bernadette always wangled herself an invitation to accompany her husband when he visited his father especially after what she overhead the last time. Maxime didn't go to the estate very often and truth be told, liked to have his wife with him. The bitchy woman provided fortification—his father didn't like tangling with her.

The logs in the sitting room had been reduced to a mound of smoldering cinders. She called the servant's quarters asking that someone attend to the fire.

"…And bring me a glass of sherry. And, oh, yes, a few of those tasty crackers and that baked Camembert cheese you served with lunch. See that the cheese is warm."

Bernadette stood before a mirror mounted over a French Provincial console table. Admiring her profile, she smoothed a blond strand into place. "So, Maxime is the father. At any rate he didn't deny it and the doctor confirmed the fool is capable. Of course, he couldn't prove it by me."

Spring, Bernadette thought. The little bastard will be born in the spring—maybe April. I'll let this little charade the Count is orchestrating play out. If the woman gives birth, I'll be ready. If she's alive that is. She heard a rap on the door, and a man entered immediately rebuilding the fire along with a maid carrying the tray of refreshments. "Madame, your sherry."

"Please let Maxime know where he can find me when he's ready to leave."

Bernadette slathered a cracker with the cheese and took a sip of her sherry. Moving closer to the rekindled flames in the fireplace, a smile slowly crossed her face. A baby, she thought. A baby with Beaumont blood would certainly ensure her lifestyle. Especially since she would know the secret of its birth. How wonderful and she wouldn't have to go through the painful, messy process of bearing the child herself. Without a baby the Beaumont blood line ceases with Maxime. Maybe she should hire her own detective. Someone to keep tabs on when the little treasure appears and the best way to bring the little darling to me. Oh, I can just see their faces when I walk in and present Maxime and his father with the baby.

Our baby.

Chapter 40

Seattle

Party time!

With his gold bars safely in a bank vault, Philip Wellington was going to enjoy himself playing Father Christmas even though Christmas was two weeks away. His new facility manager directed caterers, florists, musicians, and decorators in a panoply of motion, color, and aromas of delicacies emanating from the kitchen all wrapped in the music of the holidays. Philip specifically asked for a rotation of musicians throughout the day so everyone could enjoy the music as they worked.

The party had been written up in the society section of the newspaper. The guests included those who had participated in solving the biggest gold robbery ever pulled off in the State. The reporter, Skip Hunter was listed immediately after Seattle's Police Department Detective Mirage DuBois followed by a Ms. Wilder and her grandfather, Clay Wilder who had been key in finding the initial location of the heist but too late as the bullion had already been moved.

While the staff readied the mansion for the party that evening, Philip visited homeless shelters donating money and soliciting a list of what would help the shelter directors in their mission. He visited Seattle's Salvation Army and the Red Cross slipping each director a large check. His final trip was to Wal-Mart where parents in a few weeks would be surprised when picking up their children's toys from layaway to find that the balance had been paid.

Late afternoon, when the comings and goings of delivery vans was at a fevered pitch, a man slipped in the front door along with a florist and asked a woman wearing an apron if there was a library. She pointed down the hall and scurried off. The man followed her directions and found the door open, a florist positioning a large bouquet of roses on a table. The man stepped to the desk, looked to see if anyone was watching. No one paid any attention to him as he laid a small box in the center of Mr. Wellington's desk. The box, wrapped in brown paper, was addressed to Gillianne Wilder. Satisfied, the man sauntered down the hallway and out the front door, his limp barely noticeable and certainly not by the harried delivery men and women.

As evening descended the glow of the mansion grew when holiday lights strung inside and out were turned on to greet the guests. There was a slight chill in the air. The forecast was for a light snow—Mother Nature adding her touch to the festivities. Cars began lining the street as guests streamed into the mansion. A gray sedan pulled up and parked behind a black Lincoln another car immediately pulling behind the sedan. The driver of the sedan remained in the car unnoticed as guests passed chatting in excitement, exclaiming over the multitude of lights dotting the grounds of the mansion where they were about to join the party. The man scrunched down, pulled his coat tight around his neck and smiled. He visualized Gilly's face when someone, perhaps Mr. Wellington, handed the box left on his desk to her—if not tonight, then tomorrow, or soon.

~ ~ ~

Skip straightened his black tie, pulled on the black suit jacket, and looked in the mirror. The engraved invitation to Wellington's party indicated appropriate dress in small letters at the bottom: Semi-formal. Agatha sat next to Skip's shoe, both checking his image in the mirror. "Okay, girl, nothing more I can do here."

At the apartment Nicole answered the door and Skip stepped inside placing a quick kiss on her cheek in greeting. Neither indicated remembering the first time they met in Paris. He greeted Maria with a hug when she emerged from the kitchen, dishtowel in hand. Asking about Gramps, Maria said that Anne and Will had received invitations and were driving over together.

The bedroom door opened and Skip's heart stopped. Gilly stepped through the open door wearing a short, black filmy skirt that fluttered around her knees, the black silk stockings camouflaging the scrapes she had sustained the day before. A black sequin halter top skimmed just below her hips, the baby bump accentuating the glow on her face and the sparkle in her green eyes. Her red hair fell in soft waves around her shoulders.

Gilly smiled at Skip as she handed him her black wool cape. He draped it over her shoulder wishing he could plant a kiss on her bare back. Happy to see the impact her entrance had made on Skip, she said goodbye to her roommates and with a wink she waltzed out the door gripping Skip's arm for support.

He hoped tonight they would both relax and enjoy themselves. He made the only reference to the event at the train station. "I still can't believe you offered Arthur Lewis a job before checking him out."

"I design clothes. You are the investigative reporter. How about I design and you investigate," she said smiling up at him.

He stole a glance at her, looked back at the road. Better watch yourself, Hunter, he thought, or you'll take her home with you right now. To heck with the party.

"Okay. I'll investigate. Just to let you know, I like the guy. He saved your life and for that I'll be eternally grateful." Keep your eyes on the road, Hunter.

Entering the mansion Skip took Gilly's cape, handing it to an attendant receiving a ticket in return. Philip Wellington quickened his step to greet Skip and the beautiful woman on his arm. While he had met her grandfather, Philip had been looking forward to meeting Gillianne Wilder but had no idea she was a new fashion designer. He thought a woman as beautiful as she would take the fashion world by storm and looked forward to watching for her new label. He told her if she ever branched out into men's clothing to be sure to let him know. He handed Skip a glass of champagne from the tray of a passing waiter. Gillianne declined and Skip asked the waiter if he would bring her a glass of ginger ale. In a flash, she had a flute in her hand. Wellington had moved on to another group of guests.

Looking for Gilly's parents, they stopped at one of the food stations—canapés featuring various fish. Gramps, champagne in hand, greeted his granddaughter at the same time her mom and dad appeared by her side. Anne said if they didn't see each other again before they left she wished them a good time. She said they would be leaving soon to catch the nine o'clock ferry but wouldn't have missed meeting Mr. Wellington and seeing his beautiful mansion for anything.

~ ~ ~

Detective DuBois spotted Skip and headed in his direction, smiling to himself. Skip the protector, guardian, lover, probably all three he surmised seeing him standing beside Gillianne. He wasn't giving anybody a chance to harm her, at least for the moment. "Good evening, Gillianne, Skip."

"Hello, Detective." Gilly leaned in, kissing both cheeks, a custom she picked up in Paris. "You're looking very handsome tonight—black bow tie and all. Tell me," she whispered. "Is that a gun I see bulging under that black jacket?" DuBois instinctively touched his hip. Chuckled. "Not tonight, but I wonder if we three could talk privately for a minute?"

Skip, watching the byplay between the two, said, "Let's go to the library. I'm sure Philip won't mind and I'm very sure Gilly would like to kick off those shoes for a minute."

Gilly nodded in agreement, took Skip's arm as he led the way down the hall.

"We're in luck—no one here and look at those couches and the fire," Gilly said moving to the fireplace stroking her bare arms.

"Very nice," DuBois said. "Lovely home Mr. Wellington has here, if you can call a house this size a home."

"Gilly, I called Mirage yesterday after I dropped you off at your apartment."

"I thought you might." Gilly kicked off her shoes, wriggled her toes, and pulled her legs up under her as she sank onto the couch.

"That man who tackled you, he saved your life. Skip told me you thought you were pushed into that oncoming train. Did you see him? What makes you think it was a man?"

"No, I didn't see … I wasn't looking. I heard the train coming into the station and had just put my notepad in my purse when I felt a sharp blow to my back or maybe an elbow, a large hand splayed … felt like a man. Wait, I'll tell you what it felt like. When they show football players practicing their hitting—they rise up against the dummy as they hit. I was falling so the contact stopped as I fell forward." Gilly stared above the detectives head as she spoke. Now her eyes focused back on the detective's face. "I think I remember Arthur Lewis tackling me but that's all. Probably when I hit my head."

"I see. Well, I had a thought—this Spiky guy, Edward Churchill—"

Skip leaned forward, elbows on his knees, one hand cracking the knuckles of the other. An action Gilly had never seen him do before.

DuBois leaned back in his chair. "We think his grandmother told him you were pregnant. Let's say he didn't buy the story you told her—the father being killed. Not long after, you get the first blackmail note … postmarked Paris. We have to assume he tracked down a plausible answer to who the father of your baby might be. You said yourself, many people at work knew you were seeing Beaumont—only Beaumont. Also not hard to learn the man is running for the Senate. So, Spiky puts the squeeze on you. Now, you get another note, but postmarked Tacoma. Here's my dilemma, or should we say what doesn't fit his MO. You thought you heard the word *bitch* yesterday and immediately assumed it was Spiky. But why would he try to kill you? He wants money. See what I'm saying? If you're dead—no money."

"You're saying I imagined it … being pushed?"

"I'm saying it's a possibility. Here's another possibility. Maybe the guy you assume tried to save you actually was pushing but the wire trash receptacle stopped your fall."

"Oh, now really, Detective, I don't think—"

Skip looked up at the sound of the library door opening. A man dressed in an oversized black suit filled the doorway, looked at the three pausing on Gilly. "Sorry. Wrong room." He turned and disappeared from view.

DuBois, instantly on his feet, trotted to the door, glanced down the hall. Several waiters with trays loaded with hors d'oeuvres crisscrossed to refresh the many tables set up as food stations. The detective backed into the library and shut the door. He and Skip exchanged glances as he sat down in the chair.

Gilly observed the exchange. "Well, it seems you two have more to talk about. If you'll excuse me, I'm thirsty. I think an icy ginger ale will hit the spot." Bending forward she slipped into her shoes and stood up.

"Skip! Look. On the desk."

Skip stood at the alarm in her voice, his eyes looking where she was pointing—a small package in brown paper.

DuBois rounded the desk. He didn't touch the package, looked up over his glasses at Gilly. "It's addressed to you." Taking his handkerchief out of his pocket, he carefully slit the tape with a letter opener lying on the desk blotter. He opened the box but the three knew what was going to be inside. They were not wrong. Lifting the spiked heart with the end of the letter opener, he picked up the folded paper underneath, again careful only the handkerchief touched it. He flicked it in the air unfolding the paper smeared with blood. He laid it on the brown paper. "Blood. He's upping the ante." Dubois said, and then read the letter to Gilly and Skip.

> "Listen, bitch, my patience is wearing out. Your stupid little business must be sucking you dry. Wire the money NOW! I don't care how you get it—beg, borrow, or steal and your secret remains with me. My pain gets worse every day. The pain you and your grandfather inflicted on me. Doctors say if I don't get the operation soon I'll lose my leg. I lose my leg, you lose your life. Spiky."

Gilly, all color draining from her face, grasped Skip's arm. It seemed Spiky knew where she was every minute of every day. She was rarely alone. Her mother, her staff, or as tonight, Skip were always with her, but somehow he managed to find her, even in a private library during a party.

DuBois called the department, barked instructions at the officer on the other end. Ten minutes passed. A squad car pulled into the Wellington driveway. Two uniformed officers jumped out disappearing in the shadows as they ran in opposite directions around the house.

The man in the sedan smiled as he pulled away from the curb and slowly drove down the street parking a block away. Two squad cars rushed past him and yet another. He envisioned the police searching the grounds for the person who left a package for Ms. Wilder on Wellington's desk.

As officers searched the property a man ambled down the street stopping to talk with a couple walking their dog. Two policemen rushed by the little group of three asking if they had seen anyone lurking on the grounds, anything suspicious moving in the bushes. The three looked at each other, shrugged, and went on chatting about the beagle preening from the attention of the man who obviously loved dogs as he crouched down to pet her. The couple said goodnight and continued on their walk. The man limped across the street, melting away into the shadows.

Chapter 41

The Suit-Dress was a hit!

Initial orders combined with new orders—delivery deadlines loomed. Gilly received daily calls from Nordstrom's and the Working Girl shop—some days more than one. The decision to accept Stacy Sinclair's offer was put into writing. All agreed it was risky but so what. The worst that could happen, they'd pull out, find an apartment, and continue moving forward.

Gilly met with Hawk in his new Seattle office to go over the deal. He had registered her label and trademark along with the copyright of her name and set the business up as a Sub-S Corporation. Thoughts of buying Stacy's business were premature, for now anyway.

Nicole practically lived at the factory. Orders were coming in so fast that Vinsenso began making daily deliveries with his van—even if it was just one item. He was trying to impress the vivacious Parisian. In the meantime Gilly updated her spring collection that won the State competition.

Market analysis accelerated. Nicole and Maria took numerous field trips to department stores and boutiques, as well as scouring magazines for the latest fashions shown by other designers, noting the colors and new trends that Gilly might want to adopt. For the most part, Gilly continued with her own ideas but paid close attention to what the girls found on their excursions. She had to be ready to swap the fall collection displays at Nordstrom's and The Working Girl with the spring line by the second week in January.

Running against the clock, Gilly was trying to keep up with the needs of the two stores as well as preparing for the birth of her baby. It was understood she would try to rest after the baby was born—taking full charge of her baby girl with only an occasional peek at the business until she regained her strength. She would work into a new rhythm of mother and business woman. At least that was the plan, but everyone knew, unless something unforeseen happened, she would be back in the fray sooner rather than later.

The business was picking up a rhythm of its own which at the time meant putting out fires—Nicole running in one direction, Maria in another. But the pair knew instinctively which one would handle what, when, and where. Both tried to intervene if there was a problem before Gilly got wind of it unless it became absolutely necessary to have her attention.

Anyone seeing the girls at work would laugh. One, or the other, or all three up at various hours of the night—a cup of tea, a glass of milk, or a soda in hand. They laughed if they happened to be up at the same time. But when an idea struck, they found they had to act or the idea was gone by morning.

Anne kept a watchful eye on her daughter. She saw signs of fatigue yet Gilly kept pushing. Agreements were signed with Stacy as to what was expected of Gilly as manager of the Working Girl—which staff would remain, and what duties were to be added to Nicole's and Maria's roles.

Two more boxes wrapped in brown paper were delivered to Gilly, the notes becoming more and more desperate with threats if she didn't stop stalling and send the money. Gilly tried not to let the others know when a package arrived. She'd call DuBois who would send one of his officers to pick it up—unopened. He told Gilly that they had no trace of the Spiky culprit. He hoped with the guy's picture front and center for all his men to see when out on patrol that someone would spot him. DuBois put the apartment on a routine drive by, the officer calling to say they had just driven by and had nothing unusual to report. Spiky seemed to be a chameleon, blending into the background. DuBois needed one break. One tip.

Suddenly it was four days before Christmas, two days before Maria's wedding. A new set of to-do lists landed on the conference table. Maria packed most of her personal things and moved them to Hawk's apartment. She was staying with Gilly, however, until her wedding night. She and Hawk had tickets to fly to Sandals resort in Jamaica for five days of rest and relaxation knowing what lay ahead of them when they returned to Seattle.

A snowstorm was in the forecast beginning late on the day of the wedding so backup plans were made to escort them to the airport. Skip would drive Gilly and Nicole back to Seattle. If they couldn't make it, they'd stay with Gramps in Hansville.

As for the wedding, thankfully, tribal custom called for a simple ceremony. In fact, historically, if a women moved into a man's family home, they were considered married. A custom Maria's mom and stepdad thought was great and adopted wholeheartedly—no wedding to pay for. The ceremony was to be on the reservation and Hawk's parents insisted on taking care of the dinner arrangements including payment. Gifts to the bride and groom were not required but they received some in spite of the custom. But gifts *were* exchanged between their parents, and Hawk's father and mother gave a gift to those attending the wedding. By custom, the bride and groom accepted the gift of two blankets from their parents.

Hawk and Maria decided on a small guest list—family and very close friends only. Nineteen guests stood up for the pair as a protestant minister lead them through their vows. Gilly and Nicole stood to one side of Maria. Simple or not, Maria and her attendants each held a nosegay of pink and white tea roses. Maria wore a simple white lace, knee length sheath dress. She had found the lace with a scalloped edge on one of her excursions with Nicole. After finishing the hem of the white silk lining, Gilly insisted on adding a few clusters of seed pearls around the neckline.

Maria let her thick dark hair full in soft curls down her back, a clip of pearls holding back her hair on one side. Hawk whispered in her ear as she joined him in front of the minister, that she looked like a Spanish princess.

The ceremony ended and the wedding party moved to one of the resort's small dining rooms overlooking the holiday lights of the garden and the waters of Puget Sound beyond—a beautiful backdrop for the intimate wedding celebration.

When the first snowflake fell, the view framed by the picture windows became a fairyland as the delicate flakes mixed with the colored lights. The snow quickly became thick and heavy. Hawk and Maria jumped into the resort limo, the driver taking off to the airport. Anne and Will left for Hansville. Skip escorted Gilly and Nicole to his jeep and headed to the ferry behind the newlyweds.

An awkward moment occurred when Skip parked in the apartment's driveway. Nicole jumped out, calling over her shoulder that she'd turn up the heat leaving Gilly and Skip sitting in his car. Words hung unspoken in the chilly air—both wanted to say so much but both said nothing. The silence became strained so Skip got out of the car and came around to help Gilly—today the start of her sixth month. Holding her arm they maneuvered the snow-covered walk to the front door of the building. She thanked him for taking her and Nicole to the wedding and quickly stepped inside leaving Skip with his hands stuffed in his pockets, snow swirling around his head.

Chapter 42

The Christmas blizzard howled through every nook and cranny of western Washington. Everything came to a halt—streets were deserted, shops remained closed; a few large department stores opened and closed two hours later—there were no shoppers. If the warning from the city's road crews to stay home weren't enough the pictures on television showing stranded cars did the trick. Luckily Maria and Hawk's plane took off before the storm gathered to full force.

Gilly and Nicole sat quietly at the little kitchen table, feet up on a chair pulled between them, Maria's chair. They missed her beautiful smile and exuberance urging them on when they didn't think they could muster the strength to tackle the next item on their to-do list.

The radio played Christmas music, the television set to mute—watching the snow piling up on the roads didn't require sound. Nicole had never seen a blizzard let alone been caught out in one. The weather brought their frenzied preparations for the move above the Working Girl shop to a halt. It was nice to enjoy their morning coffee sitting at the table rather than taking a sip as they dashed past their mug on the counter.

"Gilly, I know it's upsetting when one of those awful packages arrives, from God knows where, or how. They just seem to appear. But, do you ever get the feeling that maybe Spiky is watching us?"

Gilly looked up. "Yes, but I didn't know you felt it, too. What about Maria?"

"Yes. Maria, too, and your mom. I've felt it so strong when walking down the street that I've turned around. But I never caught anyone staring at me."

"I've done the same thing. Sometimes I stop, look in all directions, but nothing. Probably nerves … because of Spiky." Gilly gazed down into the black liquid as she ran her finger around the top of the mug.

Nicole watched her sensing there was more than the blowing snow outside on her friend's mind. "It was nice of Skip to squire us around yesterday—back and forth from the wedding."

"Nicole, I don't know how to act around him."

"I wish you'd get over this silly idea of yours that you don't deserve his attention. The guy is obviously crazy about you but he's afraid to make a move."

"It's more than that. I'm carrying another man's baby. How can I ask him to understand when I don't understand myself? How could I have been so naïve? We were beginning to have feelings for each other when I left for Paris. And, what do I do when the first Frenchman comes my way?"

"Stop it, Gilly. Maxime was not just any old Frenchman. He targeted you. He wasn't honest with you. Any woman would have been caught off guard with the attention he was throwing your way."

""That's just it. I don't want to be *any woman*. I'm starting a business. Maybe I'm not up to it. Look what we're planning to do the next few days ... moving to a new place I can't afford, managing a store ... I've never managed a store ... dragging you and Maria along with me."

"You're not *dragging* us. Maria and I believe in you. We've talked about it. Yes, we have."

Gilly arched her brows at the thought that Maria and Nicole had discussed the deal with Stacy without her. She smiled. "I'm glad you have. If you two didn't pull out already, I guess you've decided to come along for the ride."

"Yes, and now I want you to stop this pity party. We can't do anything else today so let's make our lists ... lists for the next six months when the business takes over the lease. I'll warm up those wicked cinnamon buns your mom transferred from her car to Skip's when we were leaving the resort yesterday. She said more were coming when they arrive to spend Christmas dinner with us."

"Do you miss not being home for Christmas with your family?" Gilly asked stretching her arms over her head.

"A little. Christmas was never a big deal. My mom said she and dad were saving up for a visit. We'll see." Zapping the buns in the microwave, Nicole took inventory in the refrigerator. "The tuna casserole and other goodies your mom prepared will be perfect for lunch and dinner. We'll be ready tomorrow morning to take on the world ... after the roads are plowed."

"Nicole, I never could have come this far without you and Maria. I love you guys." Gilly's eyes filled with tears. She let them spill over her lids sliding down to her bathrobe. Looking at Nicole, she felt such love for her. Her hand resting on her belly she felt the baby girl kick, anxious to join her mother's world.

The blizzard eased off by mid-afternoon, the sunshine cutting through the storm clouds before setting behind the mountains. The day had been productive. Christmas music filled the little apartment with holiday warmth as they tackled the list of what had to be done over the next week, then the next month, and then the big picture—redoing the little shop to represent their line of clothes bursting out onto the fashion world's stage.

~ ~ ~

By mid-week Stacy and her husband had packed up their personal belongings leaving the second floor cleaned up and available for Gilly to make the move before the New Year's holiday. Maria and Hawk were back in the city, their olive skin sporting a deepened level of tan from the sun.

Moving day was upon them before they knew it. Anne, Will, and Gramps borrowed a van to help with the move. Gramps and Gilly were stationed in the new apartment, Gramps waving his arms directing where items were to be placed from Gilly's detailed drawing as she unpacked the cartons as they appeared. Braving the snow banks, the move was soon accomplished. Nicole had called Skip putting the idea into his head that if he dropped by at a certain time, he would be more than welcome.

After the last load everyone collapsed—a futon, two folding chairs, and a few pillows on a throw rug. Skip sauntered in with a cooler. Prepared, he pulled out a champagne bottle and a new set of crystal flutes for the occasion, the first of many he added. Popping the cork, letting it fly up to the high-beamed ceiling, he poured the bubbly and pulled out a small bottle of ginger ale for Gilly filling her flute.

"Here's to the successful launch of something big and I'm not just referring to big mamma over there," he said smiling.

"Mom, with the wedding and the move I forgot to tell you about Arthur Lewis."

"He's the man who tackled you at the train station? Saved your life."

"Yes, but what she evidently forgot to tell you, Anne," Skip said frowning at Gilly, "Is that your daughter offered him a job to take care of the books."

"What? I'm out of a job?" Anne said feigning surprise. "Not even a pink slip? Just out?" she chuckled.

"Mom, we're crazy busy—" Gilly smiled at Maria. Crazy busy were two words the girls had used often to describe their life at the fashion academy.

"I know *you're* crazy busy," Anne said. "I about had a stroke when I saw the box full of orders, receipts, bills, check stubs ... I don't know what all. When does this savior Arthur Lewis ride to my rescue?"

"January second. One o'clock. Two days a week to start."

"She wants to be sure Lewis can add two and two." Skip said. "At the hospital he said he was an out-of-work accountant." Skip popped another cork passing the bottle to Gramps to refill his glass.

"I'll hand him what will pass as my *keeping of the books*, then I resign."

"You're resignation will sadly be accepted but you're duties as visitor with an occasional pot of chicken stew are still expected to be carried out. Agreed?" Gilly, leaned over to kiss her mother's cheek.

"Agreed, sweetie."

"Nicole, we have to start ramping up our sales effort. What do you think about Gabrielle?" Gilly asked. "Do you think she'd like to join us? She indicated she would that last day when we were at the café ... seems so long ago."

"That's a great idea. Let's call her ... wish her a Happy New Year and to get her butt to Seattle on the next flight."

Everyone laughed. The darnedest words came from that sweet French girl's mouth. Sweet words were not always the case. Gilly had heard her let fly at Vinsenso if she caught a flaw at the factory. Of course, everyone thought Gabrielle was a good idea and hoped she would join the little company. Now that Maria was living with Hawk, another person around would help so Gilly was never alone. If only that detective could find Spiky.

"This apartment, if you can call it that, is pretty rustic," Will said walking around the living room with his champagne glass. "The oak floor boards could be brought back with a good sanding and several coats of polyurethane." He peeked into the space with a green refrigerator, black stove and porcelain sink—all looked old. "Seems the Sinclair's divided the second floor in two with this wall. Living this side leaving the other for storage, I guess. Empty now. You said you were going to use it as the studio—those big windows will give you plenty of light. Bet there's red brick on that outside wall."

Anne smiled at her husband. With his years of construction experience he saw the potential where someone with little or no experience would say it was beyond repair.

"I know, Dad," Gilly said sitting on one end of the futon Maria's mother had donated for the previous apartment, stretching her legs out. "The heat works and the pipes don't bang too loud —toasty in here. And, I tried the water—good pressure. But, the first plan of attack is the shop—new paint job, indirect lighting—start creating the atmosphere, environment to show off our collection. Second, a place for the baby—should have enough time to accomplish both projects."

"I can lend a hand on weekends, maybe more." Will turned to look at his daughter. She was staring at him. Did she hear right? A smile spread across his face. "Well, if you're mother's going to be here with chicken stew, I don't want to stay home and eat alone."

Gilly looked at her mom who was as surprised as she at her husband's offer.

"Hey, what about me?" Gramps said grasping his heart, hurt to the core. "I can still swing a paintbrush, not too good with the hammer. Hit my thumb yesterday. Hurts like the devil."

"I guess I'd better start the grocery list on the way home tonight," Anne said.

Coco jumped up on Gilly's lap, decided it was no longer comfortable, took a look at Nicole and gently stepped to her lap, purring as she curled into a ball.

"Maria, I think it's time for us to leave," Hawk said, stretching as he extended his hand to his wife. "I'm maxed out, no time to help you guys, with my new office, new apartment, and a new wife who demands my constant attention."

Swinging into Hawk's arms, she planted a noisy kiss on his lips. "And don't you forget it, mister."

Chapter 43

By mid-January Gabrielle Dupont had arrived in Seattle bringing a list of buyers, a treasure trove of contacts she had collected over the two years she had worked with several fashion houses in Paris. At the onset of her career, she had dreamed of starting her own business but never had the courage. When she became Gilly's agent she immediately saw the young woman's drive and hoped one day to join her in the States.

Gabby liked the independent American, and thought American men rugged and good looking. They expected a woman to be self-sufficient. At thirty-eight, she didn't appreciate the way many Frenchmen put her down, scoffed at her desire for a career. In her twenties her goal was to be a designer, but she soon learned her knack at sales was far superior to that of her design skills.

With the spring collection now on display at Nordstrom's and downstairs in the Working Girl, Gabby began a full assault on buyers with the aid of Maria's lookbooks. They were still working from a season behind *but* were ready with the fall collection to be debuted at the March event. It wasn't a big event, nothing like New York, but the fledgling company was learning—talking to customers who came into the Working Girl shop, noting their reactions to the line, their likes, dislikes, what they were looking to buy.

On Thursday nights for the next month, the girls shut the shop's doors, pulled a curtain over the large storefront windows, pulled racks of clothes away from the section to be tackled, and pulled out the paint buckets.

Taking the early Friday morning ferry, Anne, Will and Gramps set to work and didn't' leave until Sunday evening. Anne kept the troops fed. Will organized the team—he and Gramps making several runs to the paint store down the block to replenish the supply of drop clothes, rollers, or paint. An unanticipated bonus—Will was a licensed electrician.

Gilly closed the shop on weekends to accommodate the worker's hours. Gabby erected a sign: *Under new management. Closed for Reconstruction. Come back Monday. You'll love the new look and the addition of the NEW GW Fashions.* The sign went up Thursday night and stayed up until Sunday night when the Wilder crew left for the ferry.

Weekend by weekend the interior of the little shop changed from sterile white to a light tint of mauve. Indirect lighting and greenery gradually transformed the environment with a minimum of expense which mainly consisted of feeding the worker bees—big pots of chicken stew or pans of lasagna, French bread, bottles of milk and gallons of coffee.

Gilly wasn't allowed in the shop during the painting. She worked nonstop in the studio designing the fall collection to debut at the March first event. With Nicole, Maria, Gabby and her mom's help muslin samples were sewn, then the samples brought to life with the wool, silk, and trims for display on the mannequins at the event.

At Gilly's last visit, Dr. Kirkpatrick said everything was on schedule with the baby but wished Gilly would ease up on her work schedule. She needed her rest. Exhilarated by the prospect her baby girl would soon make her appearance, Gilly stopped at a second hand shop. Seeing they had everything she wanted, she called Hawk who enlisted Skip. The two men drove up in front of the shop in a U-Haul. Gilly laughed as they entered, surprised to see Skip, but grateful for his help. Hawk gave her a hug and asked, "Okay, big mama, where's the loot?"

"Hey watch your language. Just because Skip calls me big mama doesn't mean you can." A big grin spread under a twinkle in her eyes.

"Is that right?" Hawk said. "Lookin like a big mama, an even bigger mama today. What do you say, scout?"

"I think you're right, chief."

"Geez, you guys are a piece of work."

"Come on, big mama, show us what goes." Hawk said laughing with Skip.

"That room divider, baby crib, chest of drawers, changing table, and highchair. And, oh yes, the teddy bear throw rug, Raggedy Ann doll, and the Elmo lamp."

"Holy cow, this kid's never going to want to grow up. Come on, Skip, let's get her loaded."

The two loaded, unloaded, and set up the nursery in less than an hour. Anne, her arm around Gilly scrutinized the result as the men stood back very pleased with themselves. The second project on Gilly's list was complete—the little space transformed into a new infant's paradise.

~ ~ ~

The two-day March fashion event was a big success. The GW Fashion's booth was beautiful thanks mainly to Maria's marketing acumen. The four girls gathered lots of information and Gabby made lots of contacts for a show in September to launch the spring collection. Her efforts were paying off. A few customers attending the show placed orders—Nicole knew she'd be off to the factory at the end of the event. Sitting around an expanded kitchen table at the end of the final day, Gabby joked that before they knew it they'd be going to fashion week in New York, maybe set up an office in the fashion mecca, and quipped that Sheridan would soon be added to the payroll. Anne brought in a pot of spaghetti. "What's this about Sheridan? Another mouth to feed?" Anne chuckled. She was spending more time in Seattle with her daughter.

Arthur, at Gilly's request kept massaging the numbers trying to figure a way she could buy the business from Stacy. He suggested making Stacy and her husband shareholders to offer a structured deal for the business. Hawk was called in to discuss the strategy that Arthur proposed. He said it was interesting and would get back to her.

Arthur topped the staircase and called to Gilly. "These flowers just arrived. The delivery man said to give them to you." He smiled handing her the long white box as Maria and Gabby stood to see what kind of flowers the box contained. Arthur held the box so she could lift the lid. He saw their faces change from smiles to furrowed brows and frowns. He didn't know the significance of the small box wrapped in brown paper tucked beside six roses surrounded with green tissue paper.

The arrival of Spiky's package laid a pall over the day's activities. Gilly called Detective DuBois and he swung by for the package. Gilly introduced the detective to Gabby and gave him a quick tour of the new space. DuBois huddled with Gilly and Maria before he left. He said he thought they were closing in; maybe Spiky was in the area. One of his officers thought he had seen Spiky but he slipped away. "There hasn't been a package for over two months. I hoped Spiky's ardor for revenge was over. But I guess not," DuBois said.

"Did you get my message last week, Detective? About my mom talking to Helen Churchill?"

"Yeah, I got it."

"What did his grandmother say?" Maria asked.

"She heard from her son that Edward had an operation on his foot followed by therapy for a couple of months, but neither he nor his wife knew where he was, or weren't saying," Gilly said. "That's probably why the notes stopped."

"I hoped he had stopped for good," DuBois said.

"Me, too," Gilly added. "But Helen then heard that the operation was botched, unsuccessful. At any rate his mother was not allowed to send Edward any more money."

"That's why this package. He needs money. I'll let you know what the note says after forensics checks it out. No florist name on the flower box. I'll talk to Arthur on my way out—get a description of the delivery man."

Chapter 44

At 2:20 a.m. Anne sat up in bed. She heard Gilly cry out in pain. Turning on the lights she found her daughter crumpled on the kitchen floor, curled in a ball, a broken glass lying beside her in a puddle of milk.

"Nicole," she shouted.

"We're here," Nicole and Gabby said at once rounding the doorway.

"Call 911. I think she's in labor. Gilly, did you fall?" Anne asked kneeling beside her daughter gripping her hand. "Gabby, get a blanket."

"Yes ... no. I felt a sharp pain and doubled over. Mom, I'm afraid to move."

"The medics are on the way," Nicole said kneeling on Gilly's other side.

"Here's the blanket," Gabby said tucking a pillow under Gilly's head.

"That's all right, dear. You don't have to move. The medics are on their way. I'll just wrap this blanket around you. Are you cold?"

Anne wrapped the blanket while Gabby swept up the glass best she could so no one would get cut.

"I'll go down to wait for the medics. I gave the directions to the back entrance." Nicole ran to the bedroom, pulled on her jeans, a sweater and grabbed her sneakers on the way down the stairs.

Gabby looked out the front window. "Anne, the EMT van just turned down the alley. Go get dressed so you can ride with Gilly. Go. Go. I'll stay with her."

Gilly grabbed Gabby's hand as her mother darted away to get dressed.

Nicole opened the door for the two medics. They asked if there was an elevator.

"No, just the stairs. Come on." Nicole led the way through the studio to the kitchen.

The medics knelt beside the very pregnant woman, took her vitals, and told her she was doing just fine. The beefy one scooped Gilly up while the other tucked the blanket around her as they headed for the stairs. Anne pulled on her coat and followed them. "Gabby, call Gilly's doctor," she yelled over her shoulder. "Kirkpatrick. The number's on the refrigerator."

"Right. Nicole and I will lock up. Meet you at the hospital." She closed the door as the medics laid Gilly in the van.

Gabby looked at Nicole. "How early is she?"

"Three weeks I think. She's strong. She'll be okay. Tell me she'll be okay," Nicole said a terrified look on her face as a tear escaped her eye. She slapped it away.

"Don't you dare cry, Nicole," Gabby said. "We have to hold ourselves together for her."

"I know, I'm sorry. Gabby, I'm going to call Skip. He'd never forgive us if something is really wrong and we didn't let him know."

"Do it," Gabby said as she ran to the bedroom to get dressed.

Nicole held the cell to her ear, her fingers trembling. "Skip, it's Nicole."

"What's happened? Is Gilly hurt?"

"She's on her way to the hospital, Swedish Medical Center. With the medics and Anne. Gabby and I are leaving now. We think she's in labor."

"Premature! How premature?"

"Three weeks. She's probably fine … it's just she's so tired."

"I'll meet you at the hospital. Damn."

"What's the matter, Skip?"

"I dropped my cell trying to pull my arm through my sweatshirt. See you at the hospital."

Nicole picked up the car keys and Gabby locked the door as they ran out.

At the hospital, they found Anne in a waiting area down the hall from the delivery room. Skip burst through the door on their heels. They all sat in silence.

Waiting.

Wondering what was happening down the hall.

A nurse stepped into the area, glanced around at the group assembled before her. "Mrs. Wilder's doctor has arrived. Are you the father?" she said to Skip.

"No. Close friend."

"I'm her mother," Anne said. "Is she … is she going to be all right? The baby?"

"I haven't talked with the doctor. It's going to be awhile. Can I get you some coffee?"

Nicole nodded yes. "I'll go with you."

She returned shortly with four cups of coffee on a tray, creamer and sugar packets, napkins and stirrers. "The nurse insisted on all this. There's a coffee station around the corner. She fixed a pot."

Nicole set the tray down on a table. She'd done all she could. She huddled into a green leatherette chair beside the others.

From time to time, Skip would stand, pace around the room, pull his hand over his buzz cut, and sit down again. His five o'clock shadow deepened.

Two hours passed and then there she stood. Dr. Kirkpatrick. She had a tired smile on her face. "The baby girl weighed in at five pounds three ounces. A tad early but they're both doing fine. Gillianne is extremely tired and I told her I'm ordering her to stay in the hospital for three full days. Right now the baby is in an incubator."

"Oh," Anne's hand flew to her mouth, fear in her eyes.

"It's just a precaution, Mrs. Wilder. She's tired, too. Give the nurses about fifteen minutes and you can see the baby in the nursery. You can stop by Gilly's room after that but I urge you not to stay long. She needs to sleep."

The doctor turned to leave, and then turned back. "The baby sure is her mother's daughter. Has a mop of curly red hair around her sweet little face. But, boy oh boy, can she holler."

Nicole and Gabby hugged Anne, then Skip, then each other. "Oh, my God," Nicole said in a panic. "Maria. We have to call Maria."

"Hurry. Do it before we go to the nursery," Gabby said handing Nicole her purse.

Glee had replaced tension.

A nurse came up to the group and asked them to follow her to the nursery.

There she was. A tiny little red-haired angel screaming her head off in the incubator then with a jerk of her tiny fists she fell asleep, totally spent from her sudden emergence into the world.

The four adults, noses a breath away from the glass, smiled at the little bundle. Nicole at the end pulled a tissue out of her pocket, dabbed her eyes and handed the tissue to Gabby who did the same, handed it to Anne who dabbed her eyes, and she handed it to Skip who held the damp tissue to his eyes.

The nurse tapped Anne on the shoulder. "Want to see your daughter?"

"Oh, yes. Come on everyone. We won't stay but we can sure say hi."

Gilly's eyes were closed when they tiptoed into her room.

Anne picked up her hand. "Gilly, sweetie, you did good. The baby is beautiful."

Gilly opened her sleepy eyes, mustered a smile and looked from one to the other and then saw Skip as he stepped to the foot of her bed. She was about to say something but closed her eyes. Anne kissed her forehead and then moved as Nicole and Gabby on either side gently grasped her hands.

"So," Nicole whispered. "What's her name? or haven't you—"

"Robyn Anne Wilder," Gilly whispered opening her eyes a little witnessing the smiles on their faces.

"Love it," Gabby said. "Now, we're going. The doc's ordered you to stay in the hospital for three days. And, Missy, don't you dare try to come home early."

"We'll be back tomorrow, or I guess it's today," Nicole giggled. "Get some rest." She lifted Gilly's hand for a quick kiss. "Oh, I called Maria. She's so relieved you're okay and … little Robyn, too. Said she'd be over soon."

"If you all don't mind I think I'll sit with her a bit. Is that okay?" Skip asked looking at Anne.

"Of course." Anne gave him a hug and followed the girls out of the room.

Skip drew up a chair, resting his elbows on the edge of the bed, picked up Gilly's hand pressing it to his lips.

He saw her eyes flutter.

He held her hand to his forehead. "I love you, Gilly." He slowly raised his head to look into her green eyes, but they were closed, her breathing even and deep. She was asleep and hadn't heard his confession.

Later, Gilly's eyes slowly opened. She was surprised to see Skip leaning in, his head down on the edge of the bed.

"I love you, Skip," she whispered. He didn't move. He was asleep and had missed the words he had waited so long to hear.

Chapter 45

Everyone's routine dramatically changed with a new born taking up residence in the apartment on the second floor above the Working Girl shop. Lists were made and changed. Schedules were set, changed, and changed again. However, Coco stopped her roaming—she had her lap back.

Gilly thrived.

Robyn thrived.

Anne stayed to help for five days then left exhausted with Will and Gramps on the Sunday afternoon ferry.

The studio was a blur of activity—chaos to anyone dropping in to visit.

But, everyone soon settled into the organized chaos. Before Will left, he installed a board on the studio wall—a white board for messages. The board served as a sign-out sheet—each person noting where they were going and when they expected to return.

The display of the spring collection in the shop's window enticed more and more women who were walking down the street on their lunch break to enter for a look at the new line. Tired of the dreary winter skies on this first day of spring they were dreaming of a hot new wardrobe.

New orders went from drips and drabs to a steadily increasing volume.

Gabby set up a meeting area in the studio where, after exciting a potential buyer with the new collection in the beauty of the shop downstairs, she took them up the stairs to her *buyer's corner*. A tall window and an oriental rug anchored the space. In the center a large coffee table, surrounded with chairs and a couch, enticed the visitor to open the lookbooks Maria had placed within easy reach.

Nicole spent most of her time at the factory, continually checking for flaws in the production process. But with Tony Vinsenso's help, she spent more and more time sourcing fabrics, trims and researching trends.

Maria switched photographers, updated the website, introduced new signage in the shop, and redesigned the lookbooks and marketing materials.

Arthur Lewis set up his computer commandeering a corner opposite the buyer's corner. Whenever he spotted Gabby breaching the staircase with a visitor in tow, he rushed to the kitchen, brewed a pot of coffee, and set the fresh carafe on a table near the guests. After checking that the mini creamers were fresh, he returned to his computer.

Three weeks after Robyn's arrival, Gilly offered Arthur a full-time position—Accounting Manager. His hourly pay, switched to a salary, was still low, but with the increase in hours he felt rich. His wife was a part-time sales clerk at a card shop several blocks away. They had no children.

Gilly staked out her area: her design tablet always stashed into her tote at the end of the day for safe keeping still leery of someone stealing her ideas, fabric swatches, Patty standing with muslin draped in one way or another, cell phone, pages torn from magazines, and Robyn's bassinet.

From time to time, Gilly disappeared to the privacy of the nursery. Her dad had restored the rocker Anne used when Gilly was born surprising her with the gift on one of his painting weekends. After nursing her angel, Gilly laid her in her crib. With a kiss on her wispy red curls she gazed at her miracle from Paris. Maxime was a distant memory. She no longer felt hatred toward him—she felt nothing for him.

Skip popped up for coffee, or lunch, a few times a week. Neither repeated the words they said to each other at the hospital. Knowing their words went unheard, each felt content to leave them that way, once again for fear they would be rebuffed. Skip's laptop was now permanently attached to his underarm. On his visits, he brought up on the screen his latest pages of the *Wellington Gold Heist Expose* for Gilly's comments. While she absorbed the additions to the manuscript, Skip played with Robyn—just one more of her *mothers*.

Chapter 46

Coco pounced on Gilly's bed letting out a screech then darted out of the bedroom. Startled, Gilly sat up as Coco leaped on the bed again crying out. Gilly flashed back to the earthquake two years ago and Coco's strange behavior racing out of the living room and under the bed for no reason. Did she sense another earthquake?

Gilly checked Robyn in her crib. The baby slept soundly. Coco darted passed her diving under the bed. Something was upsetting her. Gilly glanced at the clock—2:38 a.m. She tiptoed out to the studio.

Flames flickered around the door to the back staircase, puffs of smoke curling into the air.

Gilly screamed to Nicole and Gabby.

"Fire. Fire. Nicole. Gabby get out."

The flames started licking at the wall.

Gilly raced to Robyn lifting the sleeping infant into her arms, wrapping her in her blanket.

Nicole stood in the middle of the studio frozen at the onslaught of the flames. Gabby grabbed her arm propelling her to the door and center staircase leading down to the shop below.

Gilly raced to her bedroom, swung her tote over her shoulder, snatched her cell off the dresser, punched 911 screaming into the phone that the building was on fire as she ran down the stairs behind Nicole and Gabby, her arms wrapped firmly around her baby.

Gilly shut the phone. Opened it again and without another thought hit Skip's code.

"Gilly it's only ..."

"Fire. The building's on fire" she yelled gulping air.

"Are you out? Robyn?"

"Yes. I called 911. Hold on I have to unlock the front doors."

Skip heard sirens. Gilly said something to Nicole. She couldn't get the door unlocked. Gabby yanked the keys from her.

Skip pulled on his pants and T-shirt shoving his cell into his pocket as he ran to his Jeep.

Gabby pushed the plate glass doors wide as two fire engines turned down the alley to the back of the building, another pulled up in front. Clutching Robyn, Gilly darted out to the sidewalk Nicole behind her. A fireman pulled them away from the entrance as he shouted directions to his crew.

Gabby pushed up the sliding bar anchoring both of the doors open.

"Ma'am, where did you see the fire?"

"Second floor. The back. There's an entrance and stairs. We came out the front."

"The stairs—"

"Stairs straight through the shop—on your right."

"Stay back. Someone will be with you in a minute."

Gabby joined Nicole standing on either side of Gilly as they watched the firemen position ladders, hook hoses to the fire hydrant, as another engine drove up the street. Horns blared, men yelled orders to one another.

Skip came running out of the alley, down the street, and up to the three women. "Everyone okay?" he shouted. Seeing them stare in horror unable to speak but out of danger, he looked up and saw a faint glow in the second floor windows. The fire must have started in the back. He dashed back down the alley, jumping over hoses, flashing his Seattle Times' badge when a fireman tried to stop him.

Flames were flaring out of the bank of windows along the back of the building. He could see that the firemen were trying to stop the progress of the fire at the studio. It hadn't reached the two windows of the apartment. If they could hold it, maybe they could keep the building from being gutted.

A Red Cross unit pulled around a fire engine and stopped. The driver asked something of one of the fireman who pointed across the street. The woman and a man wearing a white vest with a big red cross on the front and back ran up to Gilly and the two beside her wrapping each in a blanket. The woman rushed back to the Red Cross van, grabbed three pairs of slipper-socks and ran back. She and the man helped the women pull on the slippers.

"Coco. Oh, my God, Coco's in there." Gilly began to cross the street.

"Miss, stop. Who's Coco?"

"My cat. Coco. Please tell them. She saved our lives. She warned us. Please. Please tell them," she yelled over the din clutching Robyn under the Red Cross blanket.

The fireman ran down the alley out of sight.

The noise was deafening—fire engines, men shouting, police sirens, more engines their horns blaring for cars and bystanders to get out of the way. The KOMO cable news crew filled the street beside the fire trucks. More engines pulled around back. The Seattle Fire Departments weren't taking any chances that a building on fire in the heart of the city might spread to surrounding buildings.

Skip ran out of the alley looking for Gilly. Spotting her he ran across the street and grabbed her shoulders forcing her to look at him.

"It's almost under control."

Gilly looked up at the windows. Flames were still visible. It didn't look like it was under control to her.

She looked back at Skip, her eyes filling with tears. "Skip, Coco's in there," she whispered.

"Stay here."

Skip took off disappearing down the alley—reappearing several minutes later with a firefighter holding something in a towel. As they came nearer, Gilly saw Coco's tail hanging limp from under the towel.

"Ma'am, is this your cat?" He pulled back the towel to reveal a very frightened Coco, shaking, singed paws, ears, tail and back. Coco opened her mouth and gave out a soft mew. It wasn't much, but she was alive.

""Yes, yes." Gilly, tears streaming down her cheeks, put her nose close to Coco's. "Good girl, Coco, Pretty kitty. I love you."

"Ma'am, if it's all right with you I'll take her to a veterinary hospital. There's one about two miles from here. I know the vet. He'll take good care of her."

Skip pulled out his reporter's business card, wrote Gilly's name on the back and circled his cell number on the front. Handing it to the firefighter, he told him Gilly could be reached on his number and that the vet better take special care of her.

Gilly cut in, "She saved four lives tonight."

Gilly felt a touch on her elbow. Detective DuBois was standing beside her. In a soft voice, looking up at the windows which were now smashed and dark, clouds of black smoke slowly dissipating, he spoke in her ear asking her to tell him exactly what happened.

Matching his matter-of-fact tone and staring at the burned-out windows she related what she knew: Coco waking her, seeing the flames around the door of the back staircase to the alley, grabbing her baby and screaming to Gabby and Nicole to get out.

"Did you smell anything?"

Gilly turned to the detective. Her eyes sharpened as she understood his question.

"Gas. A strong cleaning liquid."

Chapter 47

Tossing and turning, Philip Wellington finally gave up on an extra hour of sleep. He picked up the TV remote from his bedside table and snapped on KOMO news. A fire engulfing a building in the heart of Seattle filled the screen: firemen shouting as they raced up a ladder laden down with equipment, firemen feeding hoses to other firemen, water gushing from the nozzles, police trying to hold back spectators.

The cameraman panned the street filled with fire engines, police cars and emergency vehicles. Wellington's eye caught sight of Skip Hunter talking to Gillianne Wilder his arm around her shoulders. She was wrapped in a blanket holding a baby. Detective DuBois stood beside Hunter. Two other women, also wrapped in blankets, were standing beside Gillianne, arms holding each other as they watched the shop going up in flames.

Wellington made a quick decision. Standing in his pajamas and bare feet, he snatched his cell from his mahogany wardrobe valet, scanned the numbers in his directory, and punched one.

"DuBois!"

"Detective, Philip Wellington here. I'm watching you on television. Would you mind handing your phone to Skip Hunter? I see him standing beside you."

"Hunter here."

"Skip, Philip Wellington. Terrible fire."

"Yes. Sorry, Mr. Wellington, I can't—"

"Wait. Skip, please tell Gillianne Wilder that my house is open to her, and her staff, and her family. I'm sure her grandfather and family will be heading across the sound as soon as they hear about the fire, if they haven't left already."

"Philip, I don't know what to say," Skip looked at Gilly and handed her the phone transferring little Robyn into his arms.

"Hello. Mr. Wellington?"

"Yes, my dear. Terrible, terrible fire. I just told Skip that my house is open to you … your staff and family. You told me at my party that you and two members of your staff live on the floor above your shop. You're homeless, my dear. Please come directly to my house when you're free to leave the scene."

"Mr. Wellington, are you sure, there are so many—"

"I've never been more sure of anything, my dear. It's about time my six bedrooms were put to use, and my staff, well, they'll be thrilled to have people in the house again. You just come along. I see DuBois is standing next to Skip. I'm sure between the two of them they can drive all of you to my place. Gillianne, tell you parents to come along as well including that wonderful grandfather of yours."

Gilly called Gramps relaying Wellington's generous offer. Anne and Will saw the fire on television and had already driven to Hansville. They were frantic, worrying about Gilly and Robyn's safety but were afraid to call knowing she had so much to cope with. They said they would leave on the next ferry to join her at Wellington's.

~ ~ ~

DuBois was conferring with the fire chief and both looked over at Gilly standing on the opposite side of the street. Mopping up operations had started. DuBois had called in his forensic team who were now methodically sifting through the ashes and debris at the back entrance of the building. DuBois signaled Skip to join him and the chief. They had a short conversation and Skip walked back to Gilly careful not to trip on a fire hose.

"DuBois said you should leave. He knows about Wellington's offer and said he'd catch up with you later. I'll drive you and Robyn, Gabby and Nicole to Wellington's."

Gilly looked at Gabby and Nicole, they nodded and followed her and Skip to his car. Gilly allowed a tear to escape as she looked over her shoulder at the blackened shop, smoke curling up from the embers as the sun breached Mount Rainier. She swiped the tear aside. "Spiky did this," she whispered in a strangled guttural voice Skip had never heard before. Twice she turned to look back at the destruction. "He'll be sorry. We'll catch him now. There's bound to be evidence. We'll track him down. He'll pay. Attempted murder. This was attempted murder! He'll spend the rest of his life behind bars."

Skip reached under her arm holding Robyn lending his support in more ways than one. His heart went out to her, letting his strength flow into her, pulling her back from the horror of the night.

Chapter 48

Skip turned into the circular driveway of the Wellington mansion, the rising sun painting the windows with gold. As Skip helped everyone out of the car, the front door opened and Philip Wellington emerged trotting down the flagstone steps. His eyes were bright, lips drawn up in a broad welcoming smile, his arms extended to the three girls wrapped in blankets, green slipper-socks on their feet.

He was followed by two women, one wearing a white apron."Here, Miss, let me take the little one," the gray-haired lady said. "My name is Gladys. I've set up a little bed in the bottom drawer of the chest in your room. Sally, please show the other girls to their rooms. You can all wash up and change. Mr. Wellington pointed you out to us on television so we tried to find you some clothes from our staff. They may not fit. We included some belts to hold up the pants. Afraid you're all a bit smaller than us," she giggled. "As soon as the stores open we'll get the proper sizes."

Gilly followed Gladys, and Sally led Nicole and Gabby to their rooms.

"Wait, Gladys...please." Gilly turned back to Skip standing in the hall looking up the stairs at her. She trotted down, threw her arms around him, whispered thank you, and then dashed back to Gladys and on up to her room.

A coffee service was set up in each room with cinnamon buns, bagels and cream cheese, bottled water, and assorted fruit. A note on each tray said to come down when they were freshened up, or take a nap if they liked.

Nicole told Sally she'd rather stay with Gabby, if Sally didn't mind. She didn't want to be alone. Within the hour, after showers and a bite of a bagel, they both scampered down the hall to Gilly's room. Climbing up on the oversized bed, Robyn asleep in the drawer, the girls sat in silence.

With a light rap on the bedroom door, it eased open and Maria scooted in, climbed on the bed hugging everyone. Tears started to flow, streaming down their faces. One thought—all their work and the beautiful shop literally gone up in smoke. Gilly reached for the tissue box, setting it in the middle of the bed. Plucking the tissues, they wiped at their tears trying to stem the tide.

"What are we going to do," Nicole whispered, quietly blowing her nose.

"Do?" Gilly said. "The only thing we four know—we get to work. Start over. But this time it won't be from scratch."

There was another soft rap on the door. Arthur stuck his head in and a woman's head appeared under his. "Can we join you?" he asked in a soft voice.

"Sure, but you have to sit on the bed." Gilly said with a smile as she blew her nose.

The door opened wide. "This is my wife Cindy."

"Hi," Nicole said scrunching over to make room on the bed. "The more the merrier."

Arthur and Cindy bent over outside the door each picking up a box, Arthur tucking his laptop under his arm. He and his wife set everything down on the floor next to the dresser. Arthur, looking at his wife, put his finger to his lips pointing to the sleeping baby. She nodded and then they climbed on the bed.

Gilly bobbed her head at the boxes, raising her hands, questioning what they held.

"I hope you'll forgive me," Arthur whispered. "It's all my accounting stuff. Sometimes I wasn't finished at the end of the day, took the papers home, and made copies in case I might need to refer to them another time. I also made a backup of the studio's computer every day on my laptop. I—"

"Arthur Lewis, just how many times are you going to save my life?" Gilly wiggled around so she could kneel on the bed and gave Arthur a big hug knocking him to the floor, everyone tumbling after him laughing that he would ever think he had done something wrong.

Robyn let out a screech which resulted in another round of laughter, and everyone leaving the room so Gilly could tend to her baby.

Thirty minutes later Anne entered Gilly's room and swept her daughter into her arms. "Thank God you're safe."

"It was scary, Mom, but everybody's okay."

Anne scooped Robyn off the bed and held her close, planting several kisses on her forehead, cheeks, and the top of her head.

"Stacy and her husband are here, in the living room along with the others. Looks like a convention down there. She wants to talk to you. Go on down, I'll take care of Robyn."

~ ~ ~

Stacy rushed over to Gilly as she entered the huge room. Philip had seen to it that the couches were pushed back, extra chairs brought in, and a long buffet table continually refreshed with snacks and drinks.

Stacy embraced Gilly then took her hand leading her to an empty chair. "My husband and I have talked over the situation with the shop, the lease ... the fire. We have no desire to renovate, rebuild. We've talked to the landlord and he indicated he was going to talk to contractors starting tomorrow to renovate the building for you to occupy. He has insurance to start the process. The insurance my husband and I carried on the business—the stock, business interruption, etcetera should take care of our creditors or close anyway. The insurance money to redo the shop is yours—do what you will with it. The landlord should be able to rid the walls and floor of the stench—probably sandblast the place. With our business insurance you can make the shop a showcase for your line, set up the second floor to your liking—a more spacious apartment and studio."

"But Stacy, the business—"

"Is basically gone. We'll transfer the lease and you'll be responsible for any outstanding invoices the insurance doesn't cover. Work it out with your lawyer and your accountant. Of course, this is all predicated on the assumption that you want to move forward. You can also say no thanks and walk away. I certainly wouldn't blame you."

Eyes darted back and forth, Gilly to Hawk to Arthur, Gilly to Nicole to Gabby to Maria. What was she going to say? The decision was enormous, the trauma of the fire still evident in all their eyes. With belts holding up pants rolled to their knees so they didn't trip, they looked like a rag-tag group. The most beautiful rag-tag group Gilly had ever seen.

But she had to think.

"Stacy, I want to say yes, just like when you came to me with your first proposal. There's even more at stake now. Can I get back to you tomorrow? I have to consult, as you say, with my lawyer and accountant." The image of the two boxes and laptop on the floor upstairs brought a smile as she winked at Arthur. "I also have to meet with my staff, get their thoughts on the best way to proceed."

"We'll be waiting for your call, won't we honey?" Stacy said to her husband. "Tomorrow."

~ ~ ~

By mid-afternoon DuBois and the fire chief had arrived at the mansion. DuBois pulled Wellington to the side. "My office informed you yesterday that Eleanor is in jail but she's making all kinds of statements trying to get released. As it stands, she's looking at a light sentence."

Wellington expelled a long sigh. "Yes, I was so informed."

"We are in communication with the Monaco Police and Detective Boisot in Paris. The investigation into Sacco's death is ongoing. They do not consider it a closed case. My officers are also working the case. As far as I'm concerned the heist started here and it will end here."

"I won't be satisfied, Detective, until I know Eleanor is on death row. I would bet all my gold that she helped Sacco fall into the sea."

"I understand. I'll be sure you are kept in the loop if there are any new developments."

The two men ended their conversation and sauntered into the living room where the convention slowly reconvened. Gilly's mom, dad, and Gramps were seated along with everyone else. They all wanted to hear what the fire chief and the detective had found. Two leather couches flanked the massive stone fireplace, stone that Wellington had hauled from his cattle ranch in Montana. The detective and the chief stood in front of the fireplace.

Stacy and her husband sat on the other couch talking quietly with Anne. A new facility manager, Gerald Sacco's replacement, had rearranged a pair of needlepoint chairs next to the couch.

Gilly entered the room and sat next to Skip at a small cherry table near a large window to the right of the fireplace.

The fire chief gave a status report on the damage. Bottom line: the building was gutted but the structure remained solid, load-bearing walls—all the walls and floors—suffered scorching and all the windows were knocked out. But thankfully the fire did not spread to any of the surrounding buildings.

Then Detective DuBois took over, hands clasped behind his back.

"What the fire chief didn't say, what I asked him to let me tell you, is that his men and my forensic team did find evidence that the fire was set. They found a timing device and an accelerant near the back door of the second floor."

Stacy spoke up. "Gilly, what I told you earlier about the landlord's insurance—he had hoped to begin cleaning up, renovating the place quickly has changed. Because the fire was set the insurance company has to investigate." Stacy's husband had a firm grip on her hand. "We, my husband and I, and the landlord have to be cleared of any involvement. You will be questioned as well. Of course, that's all silly," Stacy exchanged a worried glance with her husband. "But an investigation could take a few weeks or even months. Only after the investigation is completed to the satisfaction of the insurance company, can the renovation begin … no telling how long."

Gilly looked from Stacy to her husband, both sitting with grim faces. Suddenly the realization of what Stacy was saying brought thoughts of moving the business forward to a screeching halt. She sought Maria's eyes. Nicole reached out to Gabby grasping her hand. Both women stared at Gilly.

Dubois cleared his throat, regaining everyone's attention.

"I have news about an arrest. Edward Churchill is on his way under police escort from Tacoma to the Seattle jail."

"Oh, that's wonderful." Gilly jumped up, surprise and relief spreading over her face. "Detective, how did you find him so quickly?" The tables had turned … maybe an investigation would go swiftly and work could commence on the gutted building sooner than she thought a minute ago. They had the arsonist.

"Well, you see, he was in the Tacoma jail. He'd been there four days on an armed robbery charge."

"But …" Gilly looked from Dubois to Skip and back to the detective. "Are you sure he was in jail … last night … how … I don't understand."

DuBois didn't answer. His eyes dark, brooding.

He continued. "As I said, my forensic team did find evidence that the fire was set."

"Yes, but … you already believed it was set … you inferred as much when we talked this morning. On the street." Gilly was standing, her eyes scrunched, palms out, questioning, trying to understand. What was the detective saying?

"It was started at the back entrance. Second floor. The floor where you live."

"But—"

"Edward Churchill was in jail.

"He could not have set the fire.

"Someone else tried to kill you."

The End

Book 2: Murder by Design

Books by Mary Jane Forbes

FICTION

Murder by Design, Series:
Murder by Design – Book 1
Murder by Design: Labeled in Seattle – Book 2

The Baby Quilt ... *a mystery!*

Elizabeth Stitchway, Private Investigator, Series:
The Mailbox – Book 1
Black Magic, An Arabian Stallion – Book 2
The Painter – Book 3

House of Beads Mystery Series:
Murder in the House of Beads – Book 1
Intercept – Book 2
Checkmate – Book 3
Identity Theft – Book 4

Short Stories
Once Upon a Christmas Eve, a Romantic Fairy Tale

NONFICTION

Authors, Self Publish With Style

Visit: www.MaryJaneForbes.com for an up-to-date list